Contents

Is the Gap Between the Rich and Poor Growing?

Is the Gap Between the Rich and Poor Growing?

Other books in the At Issue series:

At ✳ Issue

Is the Gap Between the Rich and Poor Growing?

Robert Sims, *Book Editor*

Bruce Glassman, *Vice President*
Bonnie Szumski, *Publisher*
Helen Cothran, *Managing Editor*

GREENHAVEN PRESS
An imprint of Thomson Gale, a part of The Thomson Corporation

THOMSON
——✳——™
GALE

Detroit • New York • San Francisco • San Diego • New Haven, Conn.
Waterville, Maine • London • Munich

For more information, contact
Greenhaven Press
27500 Drake Rd.
Farmington Hills, MI 48331-3535
Or you can visit our Internet site at http://www.gale.com

LIBRARY OF CONGRESS CATALOGING-IN-PUBLICATION DATA

Is the gap between the rich and poor growing? / Robert Sims, book editor.
  p. cm. — (At issue)
Includes bibliographical references and index.
ISBN 0-7377-2701-2 (lib. : alk. paper) — ISBN 0-7377-2702-0 (pbk. : alk. paper)
  1. Income distribution—United States. 2. Rich people—United States.
3. Poor—United States. 4. Equality—United States. 5. United States—Economic policy—2001– . I. Sims, Robert. II. At issue (San Diego, Calif.)
HC110.I5I8 2006
339.2'2'0973—dc22   2005046117

Printed in the United States of America

Introduction

Some people are concerned about the possibility that economic inequality is growing in the United States. An increasing gap between the rich and the poor, they argue, creates fear and resentment between the classes, which weakens American society. Further, accelerating economic inequality could indicate that not everyone has the same access to opportunities in the country known as the land of opportunity. However, there are also many people who do not believe that economic inequality is growing in the United States. They argue that more Americans are thriving economically now than at any previous time in history and that the opportunities to prosper are increasing. At the root of this debate over economic inequality is the question of what is the best way to ensure that all Americans are able to achieve financial security and even prosperity.

Conservatives argue that protecting economic freedom and the free market is essential if all Americans are to have the opportunity for economic success. According to their view, a government that allows a free market and promotes unlimited competition in the private sector provides the greatest opportunities for widespread prosperity. A free market motivates people to continually strive to improve and innovate and develop new products because they face few governmental limitations on their productivity and profits.

As entrepreneurs develop their businesses and create wealth, conservatives assert, they are able to provide opportunities for other people in the form of jobs and investments. A free market that promotes production, competition, and consumer confidence thus leads to greater prosperity and a growing middle class that is able to take advantage of these job and investment opportunities. Since the health of a society is often determined by the size of the middle class and the hopes of the lower class, conservatives believe that expanding the free market offers the best way to create a stable and prosperous American society.

One of the major ways conservatives seek to protect the free market is to limit taxes and regulations, which they believe stunts economic growth and stifles the innovation of those who have the capital to invest in entrepreneurial ventures that could spur the economy and prosper everyone—including the wealthy, the middle class, and the poor. Conservatives do not view the large concentration of wealth that exists in relatively few hands in the United States as a problem. As author Richard T. Gill states, "Large incomes, whether in the hands of private individuals or corporations, supply most of the funds for private investment in all market societies."

In contrast with conservative ideology, liberals argue that the free market and laissez-faire government policies do not produce a prosperous economy with greater opportunities for all classes, but instead create a rigid economy in which the rich become richer and the poor stay poor. Liberals assert that in the United States, upward economic mobility has declined in recent years and increasingly fewer people can make it to the top of the economic ladder based on hard work and ingenuity. A special report about the U.S. economy from the *Economist* magazine states that "A person born in the top fifth [of the economy] is over five times as likely to end up at the top as a person born into the bottom fifth." Instead of creating more jobs and opportunities for the poor and middle class, some liberals state, free market competition has caused many corporations to downsize and provide fewer employment opportunities.

Most liberals concede that the United States is a prosperous nation due in large part to free market capitalism, but many also believe that the free market has flaws that have left many poor or struggling to pay for rising health care, child care, and housing expenses. In order to meet these increasing expenses, liberals argue, the government should use its authority to promote social justice by regulating the free market and implementing new governmental programs to provide a greater safety net for the unemployed, the sick, and the working poor. To fund these programs, the tax increases conservatives abhor are necessary.

Liberals view governmental programs as a vital way to provide a modicum of financial security to otherwise financially unstable families. Further, they argue that government programs such as Social Security, welfare, and the G.I. Bill have helped many poor and working class people to achieve middle class status. For example, the G.I. Bill was enacted in 1944 to provide World War II veterans with tuition for college or vocational education in addition to one year of unemployment compensation. The bill also provided low-interest home loans for veterans. A modified version of the bill, now called the Montgomery G.I. Bill, is still on the books today. According to many liberals, the G.I. Bill put the American dream within reach of many servicemen and women because it allowed many poor people to attain assets such as an education and a home that would not have be available to them without the helping hand of the government. They argue similarly that Social Security and welfare programs have provided financial relief to many poor families and prevented them from slipping into destitution. The extent to which the U.S. government should intervene in people's financial lives is among the issues explored in *At Issue: Is the Gap Between the Rich and Poor Growing?*, in which the authors examine many aspects of the debate over economic inequality.

1

Economic Inequality Has Accelerated

Paul Krugman

Paul Krugman is a professor of economics and international affairs at Princeton University and has been a columnist for the New York Times *since 1999.*

America is a society of haves and have-nots. Income inequality continues to grow, upward mobility has declined, and American society has taken on the rigid characteristics of a caste system. The American dream of achieving more than the previous generation has all but disappeared. Thirty years ago America was a relatively middle-class society, but it has since entered a new Gilded Age in which the rich grow richer and the poor grow poorer.

The other day I found myself reading a leftist rag that made outrageous claims about America. It said that we are becoming a society in which the poor tend to stay poor, no matter how hard they work; in which sons are much more likely to inherit the socioeconomic status of their father than they were a generation ago.

The name of the leftist rag? *Business Week*, which published an article titled "Waking Up From the American Dream." The article summarizes recent research showing that social mobility in the United States (which was never as high as legend had it) has declined considerably over the past few decades. If you put that research together with other research that shows a drastic increase in income and wealth inequality, you reach an uncomfortable conclusion: America looks more and more like a class-ridden society.

And guess what? Our political leaders are doing everything they can to fortify class inequality, while denouncing anyone who complains—or even points out what is happening—as a practitioner of "class warfare."

> *Our political leaders are doing everything they can to fortify class inequality, while denouncing anyone who complains—or even points out what is happening—as a practitioner of 'class warfare.'*

Let's talk first about the facts on income distribution. Thirty years ago we were a relatively middle-class nation. It had not always been thus: Gilded Age America was a highly unequal society, and it stayed that way through the 1920s. During the 1930s and '40s, however, America experienced what the economic historians Claudia Goldin and Robert Margo have dubbed the Great Compression: a drastic narrowing of income gaps, probably as a result of New Deal [Depression relief programs] policies. And the new economic order persisted for more than a generation: Strong unions; taxes on inherited wealth, corporate profits and high incomes; close public scrutiny of corporate management—all helped to keep income gaps relatively small. The economy was hardly egalitarian, but a generation ago the gross inequalities of the 1920s seemed very distant.

A New Gilded Age

Now they're back. According to estimates by the economists Thomas Piketty and Emmanuel Saez—confirmed by data from the Congressional Budget Office—between 1973 and 2000 the average real income of the bottom 90 percent of American taxpayers actually fell by 7 percent. Meanwhile, the income of the top 1 percent rose by 148 percent, the income of the top 0.1 percent rose by 343 percent and the income of the top 0.01 percent rose 599 percent. (Those numbers exclude capital gains, so they're not an artifact of the stock-market bubble.) The distribution of income in the United States has gone right back to Gilded Age levels of inequality.

Never mind, say the apologists, who churn out papers with titles like that of a 2001 Heritage Foundation [a conservative think tank] piece, "Income Mobility and the Fallacy of Class-Warfare Arguments." America, they say, isn't a caste society—people with high incomes this year may have low incomes next year and vice versa, and the route to wealth is open to all. That's where those commies at *Business Week* come in: As they point out (and as economists and sociologists have been pointing out for some time), America actually is more of a caste society than we like to think. And the caste lines have lately become a lot more rigid.

The myth of income mobility has always exceeded the reality: As a general rule, once they've reached their 30s, people don't move up and down the income ladder very much. Conservatives often cite studies like a 1992 report by Glenn Hubbard, a Treasury official under the elder Bush [George H.W. Bush] who later became chief economic adviser to the younger Bush [George W.], that purport to show large numbers of Americans moving from low-wage to high-wage jobs during their working lives. But what these studies measure, as the economist Kevin Murphy put it, is mainly "the guy who works in the college bookstore and has a real job by his early 30s." Serious studies that exclude this sort of pseudo-mobility show that inequality in average incomes over long periods isn't much smaller than inequality in annual incomes.

It is true, however, that America was once a place of substantial intergenerational mobility: Sons often did much better than their fathers. A classic 1978 survey found that among adult men whose fathers were in the bottom 25 percent of the population as ranked by social and economic status, 23 percent had made it into the top 25 percent. In other words, during the first thirty years or so after World War II, the American dream of upward mobility was a real experience for many people.

Caste Society

Now for the shocker: The *Business Week* piece cites a new survey of today's adult men, which finds that this number has dropped to only 10 percent. That is, over the past generation upward mobility has fallen drastically. Very few children of the lower class are making their way to even moderate affluence. This goes along with other studies indicating that rags-to-riches stories have become vanishingly rare, and that the correlation between fathers' and sons' incomes has risen in recent decades. In modern America, it seems, you're quite likely to stay in the social and economic class into which you were born.

Business Week attributes this to the "Wal-Martization" of the economy, the proliferation of dead-end, low-wage jobs and the disappearance of jobs that provide entry to the middle class. That's surely part of the explanation. But public policy plays a role—and will, if present trends continue, play an even bigger role in the future.

> *The myth of income mobility has always exceeded the reality: As a general rule, once they've reached their 30s, people don't move up and down the income ladder very much.*

Put it this way: Suppose that you actually liked a caste society, and you were seeking ways to use your control of the government to further entrench the advantages of the haves against the have-nots. What would you do?

One thing you would definitely do is get rid of the estate tax, so that large fortunes can be passed on to the next generation. More broadly, you would seek to reduce tax rates both on corporate profits and on unearned income such as dividends and capital gains, so that those with large accumulated or inherited wealth could more easily accumulate even more. You'd also try to create tax shelters mainly useful for the rich. And more broadly still, you'd try to reduce tax rates on people with high incomes, shifting the burden to the payroll tax and other revenue sources that bear most heavily on people with lower incomes.

Meanwhile, on the spending side, you'd cut back on healthcare for the poor, on the quality of public education and on state aid for higher education. This would make it more difficult for people with low incomes to climb out of their difficulties and acquire the education essential to upward mobility in the modern economy.

And just to close off as many routes to upward mobility as possible, you'd do everything possible to break the power of unions, and you'd privatize government functions so that well-paid civil servants could be replaced with poorly paid private employees.

16

It all sounds sort of familiar, doesn't it?

Where is this taking us? Thomas Piketty [professor of economics in Paris, France] whose work with Saez [professor of economics, University of California–Berkeley] has transformed our understanding of income distribution, warns that current policies will eventually create "a class of rentiers in the U.S., whereby a small group of wealthy but untalented children controls vast segments of the US economy and penniless, talented children simply can't compete." If he's right—and I fear that he is—we will end up suffering not only from injustice, but from a vast waste of human potential.

Goodbye, Horatio Alger.[1] And goodbye, American Dream.

1. Horatio Alger (1832–1899) was an American author who wrote boys' adventure series. His young heroes triumph over adversity through a combination of sheer will, luck, and tenacity as they advance in their chosen careers.

2

Reports of Economic Inequality Are Greatly Exaggerated

Robert Rector

Robert Rector is senior research fellow in domestic policy studies at the Heritage Foundation, a public policy research institution.

Although U.S. Census Bureau figures indicate that poverty and inequality continue to grow, their reporting is an inaccurate and unreliable assessment of poverty levels in the United States. In its calculations of income distribution, the Census Bureau ignores the taxes that people in the top quintile of earners pay, as well as the millions of dollars in social safety-net benefits that are funneled to the poor and the destitute. In addition, the millions of people who fall near or under the official poverty line would not be considered destitute by international standards. Most have adequate food, clothing, and shelter, and in fact, many considered poor own TVs and DVD players as well as cars and homes. Although some poor families do suffer from hunger, it is usually temporary. The U.S. Census Bureau has thus exaggerated the extent of poverty and economic inequality in the United States.

Poverty is a lagging economic indicator. Formal recessions (periods in which the whole economy is shrinking) usually last less than one year. However, the poverty rate almost always continues to rise for several years after a recession ends. The last recession officially ended—and overall economic growth resumed—in November 2001, but the poverty rate continued to rise in the two subsequent years: 2003 and 2004. This cycle follows the normal economic pattern that has occurred in most prior recessions.

The recent recession was comparatively mild and had a limited impact on poverty, especially child poverty. Overall, the increase in poverty resulting from the recent economic downturn has been half the increase that occurred in the last two recessions.

In the recession that began in 1980, the poverty rate of all persons rose by 3.3 percentage points over three years. In the recession that began in 1990, the poverty rate rose by 2.0 percentage points. By contrast, in the most recent recession, poverty among all persons rose by only 1.2 percentage points over three years.

The impact of the recent recession on child poverty has been modest. In the 1980 recession, child poverty rose 5.5 percentage points over three years. In the 1990 recession, child poverty rose 2.7 percentage points. By contrast, during the most recent recession, child poverty rose only 1.6 percentage points over three years.

The newly released census figures also provide evidence of the success of the welfare reform enacted in 1996. For a quarter of a century prior to welfare reform, the black child poverty rate remained frozen near 42 percent. In the years after welfare reform, black child poverty plummeted, reaching 30 percent in 2001—the lowest level in U.S. history. In 2003, the black child poverty rate rose, but was still at the comparatively low level of 33.6 percent. Despite the recession, nearly one million black children have been raised out of poverty since the welfare reform of 1996.

Health Insurance

The new Census Bureau report shows an increase in the number of persons without health insurance. However, the census count of the "uninsured" appears unreliable. Historically, census figures are significantly higher than the "uninsured" count in other government surveys, such as the Survey of Income and Program Participation (SIPP) and the Medical Expenditure Panel Survey (MEPS). The inaccuracy of the census count of the uninsured may be due, in part, to its undercount of Medicaid

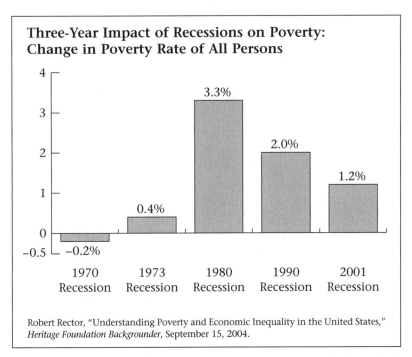

Three-Year Impact of Recessions on Poverty:
Change in Poverty Rate of All Persons

Robert Rector, "Understanding Poverty and Economic Inequality in the United States," *Heritage Foundation Backgrounder*, September 15, 2004.

enrollments. In 2003, 53 million persons were enrolled in Medicaid but the census reported only 35.6 million enrollees. Medicaid enrollments have expanded dramatically in recent years but the census figures have failed to reflect this increase. . . . Year after year, the gap between actual Medicaid enrollments and the census numbers grows larger.

The Gap Between the Rich and the Poor

The census report also contains the income distribution figures that serve as the foundation for most class warfare rhetoric. The Census Bureau measures income distribution by ranking U.S. households according to income and then dividing them into fifths (or "quintiles"). The share of total income going to each quintile is then measured. Superficially, the census figures show a high level of inequality. In 2003, the census reported that the top fifth of households had 49.8 percent of the total income, while the bottom fifth had only 3.4 percent. Thus, the top quintile appeared to have $14.60 in income for every $1.00 in the bottom quintile.

These figures are misleading for three reasons. First, they ignore taxes. Second, they ignore nearly all of the $750 billion in social safety net benefits received by low-income and elderly persons. Third, the census' fifths or quintiles do not contain equal numbers of persons. The top quintile actually has 70 percent more people than the bottom quintile. If taxes and safety net benefits are taken into account and the quintiles are adjusted so that each contains one-fifth of the population, the apparent gap between the top and the bottom quintiles shrinks dramatically—the ratio of the income of the top quintile to that of the bottom quintile falls from $14.60 to $1.00 down to $4.21 to $1.00.

What Is Poverty?

The Census Bureau reports that 35.9 million persons "lived in poverty" in 2003. To understand poverty in America, it is important to look behind these numbers and examine the actual living conditions of the individuals the government deems to be poor. For most Americans, the word "poverty" suggests destitution—an inability to provide a family with nutritious food, clothing, and reasonable shelter. Yet only a small number of the millions of persons classified as "poor" by the Census Bureau fit that description. Although real material hardship certainly does occur, it is limited in scope and severity. Most of America's "poor" live in material conditions that would be judged as comfortable or well off just a few generations ago.

The following facts about persons defined as "poor" by the Census Bureau are taken from various government reports:

- Forty-six percent of all poor households own their own homes. The average home owned by persons classified as "poor" by the Census Bureau is a three-bedroom house with one-and-a-half baths, a garage, and a porch or patio.
- Seventy-six percent of poor households have air conditioning. By contrast, 30 years ago, only 36 percent of the entire U.S. population enjoyed air conditioning.
- Only 6 percent of poor households are overcrowded. More than two-thirds have more than two rooms per person.
- The average poor American has more living space than the average individual living in Paris, London, Vienna, Athens, and other cities throughout Europe. (These comparisons are to the *average* citizens in foreign countries, not to those classified as poor.)
- Nearly three-quarters of poor households own a car; 30 percent own two or more cars.

- Ninety-seven percent of poor households have a color television. Over half own two or more color televisions.
- Seventy-eight percent of America's poor own a VCR or DVD player; 62 percent have cable or satellite TV reception.
- Seventy-three percent of America's poor own microwave ovens; more than half have a stereo; and one-third have an automatic dishwasher.

As a group, America's poor are far from being chronically undernourished. The average consumption of protein, vitamins, and minerals is virtually the same for poor and middle-class children and, in most cases, is well above recommended norms. Poor children actually consume more meat than do higher-income children and have average protein intakes that are 100 percent above recommended levels. Most poor children in America today are, in fact, super-nourished and grow up to be, on average, one inch taller and 10 pounds heavier than the GIs who stormed the beaches of Normandy in World War II.

> *To understand poverty in America, it is important to look behind these numbers and examine the actual living conditions of the individuals the government deems to be poor.*

Although the poor are generally well nourished, some poor families do experience hunger—meaning a temporary discomfort due to food shortages. According to the U.S. Department of Agriculture, in 2002, 13 percent of poor families and 2.6 percent of poor children experienced hunger at some point during the year. In most cases, their hunger was short term. Eighty-nine percent of the poor reported that their families had "enough" food to eat, while only 2 percent said they "often" did not have enough to eat.

Overall, the typical American defined as poor by the government has a car, air conditioning, a refrigerator, a stove, a clothes washer and dryer, and a microwave. He has two color televisions, cable or satellite TV reception, a VCR or DVD player, and a stereo. He is able to obtain medical care. His home is in good repair and is not overcrowded. By his own report, his family is not hungry and he had sufficient funds in the past year to meet his family's essential needs. Although this individual's life is not opulent, it is equally far from the popular images of dire poverty conveyed by the press, activists, and politicians.

> // Most poor children in America . . . are, in fact, super-nourished and grow up to be, on average, one inch taller and 10 pounds heavier than the GIs who stormed the beaches of Normandy in World War II. //

Of course, the living conditions of the average poor American should not be taken as representing all the poor. There is actually a wide range in living conditions among the poor. For example, over a quarter of poor households have cell phones and telephone answering machines, but at the other extreme, approximately one-tenth have no phone at all. While the majority of poor households do not experience significant material problems, roughly a third do experience at least one problem such as overcrowding, temporary hunger, or difficulty obtaining medical care. However, even in households in which such problems do occur, the hardship is generally not severe by historic or international standards.

Reducing Poverty

The best news is that remaining poverty can readily be reduced further, particularly among children. There are two main reasons that American children are poor: Their parents don't work much, and fathers are absent from the home. In good economic times or bad, the typical poor family with children is supported by only 800 hours of work each year: That amounts to 16 hours of work per week. If work in each family were raised to 2,000 hours per year—the equivalent of one adult working 40 hours per week throughout the year—nearly 75 percent of poor children would be lifted out of official poverty.

Father absence is another major cause of child poverty. Nearly two-thirds of poor children reside in single-parent homes. Each year, an additional 1.3 million children are born out of wedlock. If poor mothers married the fathers of their children, almost three-quarters would immediately be lifted out of poverty.

If welfare could be turned around to really require work and to encourage marriage, remaining poverty would drop quickly.

The recent Census Bureau report substantially exaggerates the extent of poverty and economic inequality in the United States. To the extent that enduring poverty continues in our society, it is largely the result of personal behavior, particularly the lack of work and marriage. Policies that require welfare recipients to work or prepare for work as a condition of receiving aid and that encourage the formation of healthy marriages are the best vehicles for further reducing poverty.

3

There Is Still a Wide Economic Gap Between African Americans and Whites

John A. Foster-Bey

John A. Foster-Bey is senior associate and director of the Program on Regional Economic Opportunity at the Urban Institute, a nonpartisan economic and social policy research organization.

African Americans have made tremendous strides economically since the beginning of the twentieth century. The end of segregation, a strong economy, and a demand for labor has allowed blacks to pursue education and attain wealth. Despite this progress, blacks continue to fall significantly behind whites in every economic category. The African American population has a much higher percentage of low-income households than the white population. African Americans also tend to own homes of lesser value. Furthermore, white households possess more than five times the wealth of black households. In addition, African Americans have greater rates of unemployment and own fewer businesses than whites. While blacks are making economic progress, it is uncertain when they will catch up to the rest of society and whether the government should intervene to address these inequalities.

John A. Foster-Bey, "Blacks Have Yet to Catch Up—Although Black Income, Wealth, and Education Have Significantly Improved, an Overwhelming Difference Remains Between Blacks and Whites in Every Economic Category," *The World & I*, vol. 18, February 2003, p. 20. Copyright © 2003 by News World Communications, Inc. Reproduced by permission.

In a 1998 article in the *New Republic*, Glen Loury, a Boston University economist, points out that even during the boom of the 1990s, compared to whites, blacks continued to have disproportionately high unemployment and poverty rates, as well as much lower family income and rates of household wealth. Other observers argue, however, that blacks have enjoyed significant improvements in both absolute and relative economic status. An April 2002 *Wall Street Journal* article quotes Harvard University demographer Edward Glaeser, who suggests that "sociologists have somehow managed to blind themselves to the fact that there were changes for the better, and in terms of historical trends there were big changes." According to Glaeser, black poverty has declined substantially over the last 20 years, while household income has increased and educational attainment has improved dramatically.

Who is right? Has black economic progress come to a halt, or have there been noticeable changes? It depends on how one interprets the data.

For those who argue that blacks have made real progress, the focus is on historical trends over long periods. Those who believe progress has been modest compare blacks and whites at a given point, such as the 2000 Census, or examine trends in economic data over relatively short spans.

Poverty

A major indicator of economic progress is the poverty rate. Between 1990 and 2000, the proportion of blacks residing in households with incomes below the poverty level declined by 15 percent. While this was the largest decline for any group, blacks still had a disproportionately high poverty rate. Based on the 2000 Census, black individual poverty in 1999 was 25 percent. How did this figure compare to those for whites and the other two minority groups? Whites, Asians, and Hispanics had individual poverty rates of 9, 13, and 23 percent. The numbers suggest that blacks are almost three times likelier to be poor than whites are and almost twice as likely to be poor as Asians.

The poverty rates for black, white, Asian, and Hispanic married-couple families in 1999 were 8, 4, 8, and 14 percent, respectively. In general, poverty rates for female-headed families are 2.5 to 5 times as large as those for married-couple families. In 1999, black, white, Asian, and Hispanic female-headed families had poverty rates of 36, 20, 20, and 38 percent.

The family poverty rates provide an important insight into why black poverty rates are so high. In 1999, single females headed 45 percent of all black families. For whites, Asians, and Hispanics, single females headed 13, 12, and 22 percent of all families. Given this, if blacks had the same family structure as whites, family poverty rates for blacks would have been 13 percent in 1999 rather than 22 percent.

Income

Between 1990 and 2000, per capita income adjusted for inflation for blacks, whites, Asians, and Hispanics increased by 108, 94, 104, and 84 percent, respectively. As a result, the gap in per capita income between blacks and whites improved somewhat between 1990 and 2000. While blacks did see an increase in their per capita income, they continued to lag far behind whites and Asians. Per capita income for blacks, whites, Asians, and Hispanics in 1999 was $14,437, $23,918, $21,823, and $12,111.

> *White households had more than five times the wealth of black households, and Asian households had more than four times as much wealth.*

The picture was very similar for household income. Black household income increased by 94 percent between 1990 and 2000, compared to 86, 90, and 89 percent improvements for whites, Asians, and Hispanics. Despite this impressive change, blacks still had the lowest average household income. Household income for blacks, whites, Asians, and Hispanics in 1999 was $39,279, $58,942, $69,602, and $44,996. . . .

There is little evidence of income polarization among blacks. Instead, all segments of the black community apparently improved their economic status. This has to be seen as very good news. The concerns expressed by researchers such as William J. Wilson that the black community was dividing into two distinct groups—a growing underclass and a thriving middle and upper class—do not appear justified.

Despite the dramatic improvement, the black population remains overwhelmingly low income. Roughly 58 percent of black households had annual incomes under $35,000. This percentage was considerably higher than those for white, Asian, and even Hispanic households (39, 34, and 51 percent). As a result, fewer black households were in the middle- and upper-income groups.

Wealth and Assets

Blacks face significant hardship. The available data indicate that the wealth gap between black and white households is even larger than the income gap.

Based on the Federal Reserve's latest Survey of Consumer Finances (SCF), the average net worth of black households in 1998 was around $64,000. The net worth of white, Asian, and Hispanic households during the same period was $335,000, $268,000, and $87,000, respectively. White households had more than five times the wealth of black households, and Asian households had more than four times as much wealth.

A major source of wealth for most families is home equity. While there were modest improvements for blacks between 1990 and 2000, according to the 2000 Census, they lagged substantially behind whites and Asians in their rate of home ownership. In 1999, ownership rates for blacks, whites, Asians, and Hispanics were 46, 71, 53, and 45 percent.

Owning a home is an important contributor to wealth, but the value of the home is critical. On average, blacks tended to own homes of noticeably lower value. In 1999, median household value for black, white, Asian, and Hispanic homeowners was $81,000, $123,000, $199,000, and $106,000, respectively.

Given the continued disadvantage that blacks experience in the labor market, it is no wonder that their income and wealth are lower and their poverty is higher.

Another source of nonfinancial assets is vehicle ownership. Again, blacks tended to lag behind the other three groups. While 76 percent of black households owned at least one vehicle in 1999, vehicle ownership for whites, Asians, and Hispanics during the same period was 92, 87, and 82 percent.

Finally, blacks tended to have lower financial assets (cash, savings, stocks, and bonds) than whites and Asians did but slightly higher financial assets than Hispanics. According to the 1998 SCF, the average black household had roughly $28,000 in financial assets, while white, Asian, and Hispanic households had $149,000, $92,000, and $26,000. On average, black households' economic status was considerably more precarious than that of white and Asian households.

Labor Market Opportunities

Poverty, income, and wealth are partially explained by an individual's experience in the labor market. If blacks, whites, Asians, and Hispanics have unequal access to employment, it is reasonable to expect that income, wealth, and poverty will be unequally distributed. In a 1996 article, economists James Eason and Manown Kisor found that between 1954 and 1993, nonwhite employment declined relative to white employment. As they write, "Title VII of the Civil Rights Act of 1964 sought to reduce racial inequality by barring discrimination in the labor market. Employment and earnings data suggest that the Act has achieved mixed results. On the one hand, the compensation of nonwhite workers has risen relative to white workers. On the other hand, the employment rate of nonwhites has declined."

According to the censuses, black labor force participation actually declined between 1989 and 1999 by roughly 4 percent. During the same period, participation also declined for whites (–1.3 percent), Asians (–6.2 percent), and Hispanics (–9.0 percent). With the exception of Asians, labor force participation tended to decline much more rapidly for males than females.

While black unemployment declined in both 1989 and 1999, blacks tended to have poorer labor market outcomes. According to the 2000 Census, black unemployment in 1999 was 11.6 percent, compared to unemployment of 4.6, 5.1, and 9.3 percent for whites, Asians, and Hispanics.

Joblessness for blacks was 47 percent, while joblessness for whites, Asians, and Hispanics was 38, 40, and 44 percent. These figures suggest that despite the robust economic expansion, the black unemployment rate was twice that of whites and Asians.

Given the continued disadvantage that blacks experience in the labor market, it is no wonder that their income and wealth are lower and their poverty is higher. Is this continued labor market disadvantage the result of racial discrimination, or are there other factors that explain the problem?

Education and Access to Information Technology

Labor economists assert that education and job skills are critical determinants of employment success and income growth. Highly educated, skilled workers tend to have lower rates of unemployment and joblessness, as well as higher incomes. A July 2002 study released by the Census Bureau found that in 1975 workers with a bachelor's degree earned 1.5 times as much as high school graduates did.

By 1999, workers with four-year college degrees earned 1.8 times the annual earnings of high school graduates. Moreover, workers without a high school diploma earned only 0.9 times what high school graduates earned in 1975, and only 0.7 what they earned by 1999. One possible explanation for the differences in income, wealth, and employment is a gap in education and skills. The digital divide—that is, a racial gap in access to computers and the Internet—may compound this gap in education and skills.

According to the censuses, blacks made impressive gains in education. Between 1989 and 1999, the numbers of blacks 25 years and older with at least a college education rose by 20 percent. During the same period, the numbers of whites, Asians, and Hispanics with college educations increased by 17, 14, and 5 percent.

Despite this impressive attainment, blacks still lagged behind both whites and Asians in their level of education. In 1999, 20 percent of blacks 25 years and older had at least a bachelor's degree. The corresponding figures for whites, Asians, and Hispanics were 33, 51, and 15 percent.

At the other end of the scale, 28 percent of blacks 25 years and older in 1999 lacked a high school diploma. Among whites, Asians, and Hispanics, 16, 20, and 48 percent had no diploma. While blacks were disadvantaged educationally when compared with whites and Asians, Hispanics had the lowest attainment rate.

Another factor may be employers' perception of the technological skills of blacks and Hispanics compared with those of whites and Asians. One measure of the potential difference in technological skills is computer literacy.

Based on the Census Bureau's Current Population Survey (CPS), in 2000, 56 percent of white households and 66 percent of Asians households had a computer, compared with 34 percent of Hispanic households and 33 percent of black households. The racial gaps for access to the Internet are very similar. Fifty-one percent of Asian and 48 percent of white households have access to the Internet. On the other hand, only 24 percent of black and Hispanic households have Internet access.

Given the needs of the modern economy, facility with computers and information technology is considered fundamental to economic success. The figures on computer and Internet access imply that blacks and Hispanics are likely to have a lower level of information-technology skills than whites and Asians do. This potential gap in computer and technological literacy may explain why racial gaps in earnings and employment continue.

Business Ownership and Entrepreneurship

Another explanation for the disproportionately higher rates of poverty and lower levels of income and wealth among blacks may be their low rates of business ownership. The SBA [Small Business Administration] produces periodic reports based on the Census Bureau Survey of Minority-Owned Business Enterprises (SMOBE). The most recent report was produced in November 2001 and provides information on minority businesses from 1982 to 1997.

> *This potential gap in computer and technological literacy may explain why racial gaps in earnings and employment continue.*

Based on the SMOBE, blacks increased their ownership of business between 1982 and 1997 by 26 percent; during the same period, white business ownership grew by 4 percent and Asian and Hispanic business ownership increased by 39 and 58 percent. As a result, business density, defined as the number of black-owned businesses per 1,000 households, increased by 4 percent. This increase occurred while white, Asian, and Hispanic business density was declining.

Despite the increase in business ownership, blacks lagged behind whites, Asians, and Hispanics in business activity. In 1997, black business density was 65, compared with 187 for whites, 251 for Asians, and 121 for Hispanics.

Moreover, the average black-owned business produced fewer sales per business and less revenue per household. Sales per business for black-owned enterprises were $91,000 in 1997 compared to $496,000 for white businesses, $391,000 for Asian, and $166,000 for Hispanic. The racial-ethnic gap in business revenues per household was even greater. For blacks in 1997, business revenues per household were only $6,000. During the same period, business revenues per household were $93,000 for whites, $98,000 for Asians, and $20,000 for Hispanics.

Economic Distance

The economic data on the four groups suggest that using the term minority as shorthand for economic disadvantage may no longer be appropriate. Asians as a minority group have much more in common with whites than with blacks or Hispanics. While their poverty rate is still slightly higher than that of whites, their household income, wealth, and education place them among the most economically successful groups in the United States. Economically, Asians have almost nothing in common with blacks or Hispanics.

On the other hand, blacks and Hispanics seem to be quite similar in their degree of economic progress. They have similar and disproportionately high poverty rates and relatively low income. Overall, though, Hispanics seem to be doing somewhat better. While blacks have more education than Hispanics, Hispanics are more likely to be employed.

Moreover, Hispanics have much lower rates of female-headed households. Given the fact that on average female-headed households have lower income and higher poverty rates than married-couple families do, this gives them another important economic advantage over blacks. Finally, Hispanics as a group seem to have been more successful at creating wealth and owning and operating business enterprises.

Nevertheless, despite periods of stagnation, the long-term economic trend for blacks has been positive. Since at least the early twentieth century, the key economic indicators have tended to move in the right direction. Poverty and unemployment have gone down, and income, wealth, and education have gone up.

While much of this progress can and should be attributed to the ending of legal forms of segregation and discrimination, much of the progress has been the result of the strong U.S. economy and its demand for labor. The last decade of the twentieth century was no exception. Blacks improved their economic status, in some instances dramatically, during this period. As a result, they were able to close some of the historic economic gaps with whites.

In the final analysis, despite the strength of the 1990s economic expansion, there are still overwhelming distances between blacks and whites, and now Asians, in all areas related to economic progress. In some areas, such as household income, employment, and wealth, blacks also trail Hispanics.

Are blacks making real economic progress? Clearly, the answer is yes. The real issues are how long will it take blacks to catch up to the rest of society and what, if any, public policy interventions would be required and acceptable to speed up the pace of change.

4

African Americans Are Thriving Economically

Steve Miller

Steve Miller is a reporter for Insight on the News *and its sister publication the* Washington Times.

African Americans are advancing economically and making tremendous strides in education and business. The civil rights movement broke down economic and social barricades, and blacks are taking advantage of the new opportunities. They are attending college and are being courted by large corporations. Many have achieved wealth and status through determination, successful risk taking, and hard work. Unfortunately, the media continue to ignore black advancement and affluence. They focus instead on the poverty and crime that plague inner-city ghettoes and portray the black community as oppressed and destitute.

The stories pop up like a man-bites-dog piece: "Minority businessman gains foothold . . . Black-owned businesses spread . . . Local black merchant seeing revenue." The headlines almost declare black success an anomaly. It isn't.

Unprecedented strides are being made on the economic ladder in black America. In the 1940s, one in 100 blacks had incomes that approached those of middle-class whites. Today, one in six blacks lives at the poverty line.

Mainstream black magazines such as *Essence* trumpet these triumphs, but most white Americans know well-to-do blacks as athletes and entertainers. Sure, Bob Johnson gets plenty of ink in *Forbes* magazine: The outspoken founder of Black Entertainment Television is a photogenic and articulate man worth more than $2 billion. But what about the Johnson family of Chicago? Johnson Publishing Co., which puts out *Ebony* and *Jet*, is worth more than $450 million.

The Wrong Image

Many in the black community are beginning to resent its conventional image as oppressed and economically disadvantaged. The raw numbers from last year's [2001] census show that blacks have made considerable economic and educational progress during the 1990s. Black median household income grew 15 percent between 1989 and 1999, compared with 6 percent for white families; and the number of black-owned firms increased 26 percent from 1992 to 1997, compared with a 7 percent increase for U.S. firms overall.

As consumers, blacks are one of the most targeted markets today. They spend $571 billion annually on consumer goods—$270 billion more than a decade ago. While travel overall in the United States increased 1 percent between 1997 and 1999, the number of blacks traveling increased by 16 percent during that same period.

Black affluence can be a hard sell, however, especially to those born and raised in poverty. "Anybody who can say they are responsible for their own success is egotistical," insists Wayne Ward Ford, a garrulous, charismatic 50-year-old Iowa legislator. He also is executive director of Urban Dreams, a 16-year-old tax-exempt program for urban youths that he began with $10,000 in seed money from the local city council. Ford grew up in Washington, where he committed strong-armed robbery and used cocaine, but luckily escaped from a violent world of crime. Now he wrestles with the reality of his success while many in his community still are disadvantaged.

Blair Walker, a journalist who lives in Columbia, Md., is even more adamant about the plight of blacks in America. "There are so many families hovering around the poverty level in this country," he says. "Granted, there seems to have been a remarkable boom in black affluence over the past couple of decades. . . ." He trails off, as if perplexed by his own realization.

A Baltimore native, Walker lives comfortably with his wife and two daughters. He is not wealthy, but he is successful. His parents, both schoolteachers, brought him up securely. But

Walker still believes his race is not faring well. "A fair number of African-Americans are starting off in the bottom of the eighth inning behind by five runs," he says, his voice flat and determined, the voice of an assured man.

A black America coming apart at the seams is a certainty among people such as Walker, who remain convinced that the destiny of blacks is determined by the legacy of racism. "The difference between a poor white man and a poor black man is that the white man can put on a suit and go to the same arenas as the black and he will be viewed much more positively," Walker says.

Black Entrepreneurship

But a new generation born after the civil-rights era has realized that corporate doors are wide open and entrepreneurs can be found in all sectors of society, even if old stereotypes die hard. "A story like *Boyz N the 'Hood* sells a lot better than an upper-class entrepreneur who takes care of his family," says Lloyd Lawrence, casually brushing his hand against an $8,000 leisure chair. "There are many more black entrepreneurs than the world knows about."

Lawrence stands in the swank showroom of Roche-Bobois, his furniture boutique in San Francisco's Market District across from Sega headquarters. Lawrence, a former Army captain, rejects outright the rhetoric of black victimhood and oppression. "All my ills were not caused by whites, and I wasn't helped by all African-Americans either," Lawrence says.

> *Unprecedented strides are being made on the economic ladder in black America.*

In the garage at his Oakland home is an $80,000 Porsche Turbo he bought recently as a gift to himself. "That was my allowance for working," he explains. "But I don't want to send any Puffy Combs message; I am not interested in ostentatious surroundings." The European furniture he sells is custom-made for the rich and famous—people such as Mayor Willie Brown, members of the Oakland Athletics, musicians and computer executives. Lawrence worked at his boutique 11 years before he was able to afford a single piece of furniture from his inventory.

Lawrence's affluence also has brought him a happy family environment. His life revolves around his wife, Cynthia, and his daughter, Ariana. "The most prevalent issue in my household is the education of my daughter," he says. "We give her computer summer camp, world travel. . . . She will have a very well-rounded education."

It's a can-do world for Lawrence. "I would be kidding myself to say that I have not been a victim of racism," he says, his face settling into a frown. "But there will always be that person who will reward excellence. While we will never eliminate racism or discrimination, I do delight in proving people wrong."

Rejecting Any System of Racial Preferences

Blacks are making money now because the business world realizes that buying power is there. The civil-rights movement brought virtually every black with any ambition to the economic table of America. Now, says Herb Strather, "we're part of the American economy, no matter what." Born to welfare recipients in Detroit, Strather eventually brought casino gambling to the Motor City. The self-described philanthropist is a self-made man. He easily can give a $1 million donation to his favorite cause—and he does. He rejects racial set-asides or any system of racial preferences. "I don't want anybody giving me business just because I'm an African-American," Strather says. "All I want is a chance."

The very idea of a handout rankles Tracy Glenn, who grew up in the University City neighborhood of St. Louis, a racially mixed area that now is one of the city's most desirable ZIP codes. Her folks were working class: Dad was employed in a computer job for the government; Mom stayed at home. At 31, the Houston lawyer already has made more money than her parents ever did.

Glenn, who earned her law degree at Boston University, anticipates the collective refrain of people who hear her success story and wonder how someone so privileged can speak to any member of the underclass. "There will be people who say, 'That's easy for her to say, she had a decent upbringing,' but, hey, that's not a reason to sit around and wait for the government or the white man to help them out," Glenn says.

She has been involved in landmark civil-rights cases, representing the white plaintiff in a reverse-discrimination case in

Florida. "Discrimination is discrimination; there is no reverse," she says. "I think that most people, and almost all of the people I know, are getting tired of leaning on race. It is who I am," she says, "but it is not what I am."

Andy McLemore Jr. of Detroit is convinced that the long-standing assumptions of the civil-rights establishment are things of the past. He refuses to buy into the prevailing belief that blacks are held back because of a racist white power structure. "I think it is tougher still for blacks, but so many of those limitations are self-imposed," says McLemore, who, with his brother and father, have built a thriving real-estate-development company in Detroit.

A trim man with a stylish mustache and a chuckling, easy manner, McLemore was born in the front room of his grandmother's home in Rocky Mount, N.C., and raised in the segregated South. "Back then, they didn't allow black doctors to deliver babies at the hospital," he explains. He lived through the civil-rights era, graduating from Mumford High School in Detroit in 1972 and Wayne State University. The history of second-class citizenship among blacks is not lost on him.

> *The achievements of black entrepreneurs mostly are overlooked by a mainstream media whose coverage continues to be dominated by stories of blacks mired in poverty, drugs and inner-city ghettoes.*

"My grandmother took me around to see the separate drinking fountains and the balconies at the movie theater where the blacks had to sit," McLemore recalls. "It was a different era that I might never have seen, but my grandmother saw to it that I did. I recall she took me to the cotton field across the street and had me touch the cotton boll, to see how hard the shell was."

McLemore has achieved the kind of wealth and luxury that Americans of all races aspire to. Today, he and his family live in a sprawling two-story Tudor house in the ritzy Palmer Woods neighborhood. His garage is full of luxury cars: a black Porsche convertible he bought new in 1997; a white Mercedes with a sunroof; and one of several Land Cruisers with the A-Mac logo on the side.

The Land Cruisers, however, caused a flap in the black community that still rankles McLemore. He bought several of them for his employees to foster team spirit, but some neighbors resented the display of wealth. Not all blacks view success as a good thing, McLemore says. "Many African-Americans feel that because of the color of their skin, they can't achieve something," he says. "They see someone else doing well, and it's jealousy all over."

Ignored by the Media

The achievements of black entrepreneurs mostly are overlooked by a mainstream media whose coverage continues to be dominated by stories of blacks mired in poverty, drugs and inner-city ghettoes rather than comfortable in success, prosperity and wealth. Indeed, blacks who have become successful within the media often help to perpetuate the notion of chronic black underachievement and the problem of racism.

"We continue the struggle," is how TV personality Tavis Smiley opened an appearance at the Georgetown Barnes and Noble bookstore in Washington last year [2001]. Smiley, dapper in a black designer suit over an olive green button-up, sat square-jawed and broad-faced. Unsmiling, he told the crowd that the ordinary routine of living is a fight for most blacks.

"The trouble is that the media look at black people as either the Huxtables or *Boyz N the 'Hood*," sighs Reggie Daniel, president of Scientific & Engineering Solutions, a computer consulting firm in Maryland. "In the end, though, it always falls back on the latter." A youthful looking 41-year-old, Daniel started his firm five years ago with two employees in the basement of his home. He now employees 110 people.

Daniel insists that opportunities for blacks never have been better and are improving every day. "These are not racial issues these days," says Daniel, who came from a blue-collar background in Milwaukee. "These are simply socioeconomic issues. And all races have them."

When Lawrence Otis Graham embarked on writing his 1999 book, *Our Kind of People: Inside America's Black Upper Class*, he knew that documenting the existence of a black economic elite would not always be well-received by the black community. "People are uncomfortable with such depictions of blacks," Graham explains. "They have a very narrow definition of being black, where you are only authentic if you are poor, uneducated, listen to rap music and the only way you should made money is to be a rap star or an athlete."

His book was derided by many blacks. Graham himself was labeled an Uncle Tom who ignored the prevalence of racism, inner-city slums and black unemployment. But Graham maintains that black prosperity has every right to sit next to white wealth. "Things are now changing in a number of black communities," he says. "Black families are moving to the suburbs. They now live and work next to white people and send their children to the same schools as white people."

> **"** *[The black community has] a very narrow definition of being black, where you are only authentic if you are poor, uneducated, listen to rap music and the only way you should make money is to be a rap star or an athlete.* **"**

Take, for example, the gated community of Woodmore in Prince George's County, a Maryland suburb that abuts the nation's capital. The dining room of the Country Club at Woodmore is standard upscale, with a sweeping view of the 65-acre lake that is the centerpiece of 18 holes of Arnold Palmer design. The club sits amid a 300-home gated development, a place that might be stereotypically associated with white, Republican churchgoers with minivans and sport utility vehicles in their driveways. In reality, Prince George's County is the wealthiest black enclave in the United States. . . .

Opportunity and Ambition

It's graduation day, May 20, 2001. In the humid, early-morning Georgia drizzle, 500 students form a sea of happy faces framed by yellow-tasseled caps, bodies draped in gowns. Carl Prather, watching the parade from the front of the Martin Luther King Jr. Chapel, knows well that his son, Carl Jr., has something he didn't.

"When I graduated, opportunities were still new," says Prather, a Morgan State graduate who now is an analyst for a Maryland nonprofit organization. "Now, these kids know how to play the game. They know how to capture the opportunities."

His son is destined for law school. "I've got to do everything in my power to keep from crying," he says. "I am so proud."

Most of the graduates already have secured at least their immediate futures. Some are going to Wall Street to work for the summer. Others, such as Carl Jr., are continuing their education at law school. All are heavily courted in a world that eagerly anticipates scholastically accomplished young black men.

Corporate allocation of minority representation now is part of the country's business culture. Anheuser-Busch Inc. will award $5 million in scholarships to minorities during the next five years through its Urban Scholarship Program. Any black business journal in any city features full-page ads of job fairs alongside advertisements for banks waiting to lend money to future black homeowners. "Our goal: One million African-American homeowners by 2005," reads one ad in a San Francisco newsletter, placed by the Congressional Black Caucus Foundation.

"The civil-rights movement created opportunity when none existed," says George Williams, an investment banker in Houston. "My bet is that my admission to Harvard was part of a plan to open the admissions window." Williams is pure Ivy League, from the sensible wire frames of his glasses to his khakis to his deliberate speech. A divorced father of one, he once agitated for black power. Today, he drives a Volvo station wagon to commute between his condominium downtown and the impressive estate he bought for his parents in north Houston. It's a modest mansion, really, with its spiral staircase just past the wine cellar and sauna.

"The life I live today is truly the American Dream," he says. The way Williams sees it, he walked through a door that already was open, at a time when the civil-rights movement broke down the segregationist barriers of the past. At 52, he's ready to say that today, "there is little ailing black America. . . . It is now just a matter of catching up."

5

American Families Suffer from Growing Economic Instability

Jacob S. Hacker

Jacob S. Hacker is a professor of political science at Yale and a fellow at the New America Foundation, a nonpartisan public policy institute.

American families face financial insecurity and rising living expenses. One of the reasons for this is changes in the workplace. Job security for both less skilled and educated employees has decreased in the past decade. Furthermore, workplace benefits such as health insurance and pensions have been drastically cut. The increasing number of women entering the workforce has also contributed to economic instability because although families gain a second income, they incur additional expenses such as increased taxes. The government should help American families facing these insecurities by preserving existing social insurance programs and creating additional ones. One promising proposal is for universal insurance, an umbrella policy that would protect families that face job loss or sudden catastrophic expenses.

Most Americans believe the economy is getting worse or just holding steady, and the number who approve of [President George W.] Bush's economic stewardship has dropped significantly from the beginning of the year [2004].

Pundits have offered plenty of reasons to explain—or, more

Jacob S. Hacker, "False Positive," *New Republic*, vol. 231, August 16, 2004, pp. 14–17.

accurately, to explain away—voters' continuing grumpiness. Until recently, the favored line was that voters simply had not woken up and smelled the economic coffee. Yet, public perceptions of the economy have remained remarkably negative, and they continue to be down sharply from earlier this year.

It's time to embrace a simpler thesis: Voters say the economy isn't getting better because, as far as they're concerned, it's not. And perhaps the best explanation for this perception is that Americans are facing rising economic insecurity even as basic economic statistics improve. In March, for example, unemployment and inflation were both low. But roughly half of Americans agreed that "America no longer has the same economic security it has had in the past," while another fifth thought the statement could be true in the future. By contrast, just 27 percent believed the poor conditions of recent years represent merely the normal downside of the business cycle.

This pervasive public anxiety is the main reason that usually sunny Americans are cloudy about their families' economic futures. . . . Put simply, the statistics pundits love to cite don't capture what most Americans feel: an increasing financial pinch that is putting them at ever greater economic risk. . . .

Financial Insecurity

The strains are certainly real. As Harvard Law Professor Elizabeth Warren and her daughter, Amella Tyagi, have documented, middle-class families confront rising difficulties meeting basic expenses—such as housing and tuition—and they are going deeper and deeper into debt as a result. They are also working longer. According to Karen Kombluh of the New America Foundation [a political think tank] the typical family spends 22 more hours per week at work than it did in 1969.

Yet, the income squeeze that families face is not exactly the same as insecurity. Insecurity is something larger—the risk of large drops in living standards caused by loss of income or catastrophic expense. And, my research suggests, insecurity is something that more and more Americans, even the relatively well off, are confronting.

The signs are everywhere. Fourteen million more Americans lack health insurance now than two decades ago. Meanwhile, corporations have abandoned "defined-benefit pensions" that offer a fixed payment in retirement in favor of more risky "defined-contribution" plans like 401(k)s. And, according to Princeton economist Henry Farber, the effect of job loss on work hours, pay, and prospects for reemployment has worsened substantially since the 1980s. Indeed, in area after area, there's evidence of a vast shift in the economic security of most Americans—a massive transfer of financial risk from corporations and the government onto families and individuals.

This great risk shift has gone surprisingly underreported. Though we've heard about economic hardship, most of the stories concern static measures—poverty, inequality, wages, joblessness. That's in large part because no standard economic statistic tries to assess the stability of family income. We know with great precision how many Americans are rich and poor at any moment and how large the gap is between the bottom and the top. But we know next to nothing about the extent to which their economic status changes over time or what causes these shifts.

> **"** *Fourteen million more Americans lack health insurance now than two decades ago.* **"**

In response, I have spent the last couple of years trying to assemble new figures on changes in family income, aided by Professor Niger Nargis of the University of Dhaka. Our research has centered on the Panel Study of Income Dynamics—a nearly 40-year project that tracks the same families from year to year and, hence, provides unique insights into how and why incomes change over time.

What has become clear from this research is that family incomes rise and fall a lot—far more than one would suspect just looking at income-distribution figures. As a result, a surprisingly big chunk of U.S. income inequality—perhaps as much as half—is due to transitory shifts of family income, rather than permanent differences across families.

This is a point conservatives love: Sure, inequality is growing, they argue, but mobility is alive and well, making any comparison of income groups misleading. But this conclusion is as wrongheaded as the image of a frozen class structure that liberals sometimes take from income-distribution statistics. Upward mobility is real, but it's usually not dramatic, and nothing suggests it has increased significantly in the era of rising inequality.

Plus, conservative paeans to social mobility miss an even more glaring problem: What goes up also goes down. And, for most Americans, downward mobility is far more painful than upward mobility is pleasurable. In the 1970s, the psychologists Amos Tversky and Daniel Kahneman gave a name to this bias— "loss aversion." Most people, it turns out, aren't just highly risk-averse—they prefer a bird in the hand to even a very good chance or two in the bush. They are also far more cautious when it comes to bad outcomes than when it comes to good outcomes of exactly the same magnitude. The search for economic security reflects a basic human desire to guard against losing what one already has.

Judged on this basis, what my evidence shows is deeply troubling. When I started out, I expected to see a rise in the instability of family income. But nothing prepared me for the sheer magnitude of the increase. At its peak in the mid-'90s, income instability was almost five times as great as it was in the early '70s, and, although it dropped somewhat during the late '90s (my data end in 1999), it has never fallen below twice its starting level. By comparison, permanent income differences across families have risen by a more modest, if still troubling, 50 percent over the same period.

> *Upward mobility is real, but it's usually not dramatic, and nothing suggests it has increased significantly in the era of rising inequality.*

The full explanation for this dramatic rise in instability is still unclear, but two causes loom large. The first, and most obvious, is changes in the nature of work. In today's postindustrial economy, less skilled workers are much more vulnerable than when unionized, manufacturing labor was more of the norm. (Not surprisingly, instability is greater for families headed by less educated workers, though it has actually risen more quickly in the last decade for workers who went to college.) Workplace benefits, such as health insurance and pensions, have been on the chopping block. And corporate America increasingly relies on part-time, contingent, and contract workers—all of whom enjoy precious little security.

The second overarching cause of increased insecurity is a

shift we often take for granted: the movement of women from home to work. As mothers have entered the labor force in increasing numbers, families have gained a second income, which most desperately need. But they've also had to take on new expenses and face the increased job insecurity of having two family members in the workforce.

Safety Net

A stunning finding from my research illustrates this double-edged effect: When adjusted to account for the expenses a family of a given size incurs, a family's total income actually falls when a couple starts living together. That's not, of course, because families in which there are two potential earners receive less in earnings. It's because they are likely to receive less in public benefits and to pay more in taxes just as their family size increase—and so their overall economic standing drops. Divorce and separation obviously aren't good for income security. But it turns out that marriage and cohabitation aren't a guarantee of it either.

All this reveals a truth often forgotten amid talk of "family values": The United States has never done much to deal with the income risks that come from having both mom and dad in the workforce—from child care costs, to the need for time off to have kids and care for sick family members, to the increased risk to accustomed standards of living that plague families dependent on two jobs. We live in a twenty-first century economy dominated by two-earner families. Yet, social protections for working Americans have changed remarkably little since the mid–twentieth century—and, when they have changed, they have usually been cut, not expanded.

This isn't a coincidence, of course. The last two decades have witnessed a revival of the American credo of personal responsibility, championed by conservatives as an all-purpose tonic to every social ill. . . . To the extent government has any role to play in this everyone-on-their-own vision, it is limited to giving people tax breaks to encourage them to save and invest on their own.

Not surprisingly, then, spending on social programs has barely budged over the past two decades, but private-sector spending, subsidized by hundreds of billions of dollars in tax breaks for retirement and health benefits received disproportionately by the well-off, has grown at a much faster clip. Indeed, private expenditures on such benefits now represent more than one-third of all U.S. social spending—an amount that, if added to public spending, would make the American welfare state larger than Denmark's.

Ownership Society

And, in fact, in the current campaign, Bush has been calling for a radical acceleration of this trend, integrating his previous proposals for partial privatization of Social Security and Medicare into a larger package of initiatives to wean Americans from their dependence on public programs. The shift is embodied in the campaign's recent theme of an "ownership society"—a shameless appropriation from left-leaning law professors Bruce Ackerman and Anne Alstott, whose 1999 book, *The Stakeholder Society*, outlined a $255 billion plan for giving all children a government-financed trust fund—in effect, making every kid a trust-fund baby.

Bush's more plutocratic notion of ownership has two parts. The first is reform of existing social programs to increase reliance on the private sector. Although Bush's plan for private accounts in Social Security stalled in his first term, he reportedly plans to revive it during his second. And Bush has already won some of his goals for Medicare reform in the recent prescription-drug legislation—which throws huge new subsidies at the private sector in an effort to increase the role of private health plans within the program.

> *The last two decades have witnessed a revival of the American credo of personal responsibility, championed by conservatives as an all-purpose tonic to every social ill.*

The second aspect of Bush's ownership society is a bevy of new tax-free accounts for everything from medical care to retirement savings to education. The idea is to encourage Americans to leave behind the semi-socialistic risk-pooling of corporate benefit plans and public programs in favor of socking away their own money. Like his tax cuts, Bush's "ownership society" would be a costly boon to the well-off, who not only save the most, but also get the largest tax breaks when they do. (Instead of making every kid a trust-fund baby, Bush has a program mainly designed to help trust-fund babies.) Worse, crippling private-sector risk-pooling and further encouraging the wealthy to disdain the public sector would make the problem of insecurity much more severe.

Conservatives demand a go-it-alone world of personal responsibility. Yet, the truth is that Americans can't cope with insecurity on their own. Private insurance often works well, but it has inherent drawbacks in dealing with big economic risks. Profit-making insurers simply can't offer reasonably priced protection to high-risk groups, provide affordable insurance for the less affluent, or require that everyone has coverage. Only government can.

> *Universal insurance would protect Americans before they fell into poverty, lessening the burden on programs for the poor and protecting the dignity of beneficiaries.*

This is not a radical or new idea. It's called social insurance, and it's already embedded in America's two most cherished programs, Social Security and Medicare. We now think of Social Security as a soft-headed social measure. Back in 1935, however, it was seen as the cornerstone of a system of basic financial security that was essential to making capitalism work. That's why the original name for the legislation was the Economic Security Act.

Today, we need an Economic Security Act for American families. It should begin with the preservation of existing social insurance programs. But it cannot end there. According to University of Pennsylvania social policy expert Julia Lynch, U.S. social programs are more skewed toward the aged than in almost any other nation. The United States doles out nearly 40 times as much per senior citizen as per child and working-age adult. The currently favored response to this imbalance is to cut spending on the aged. But, rather than slashing existing protections, we should instead work to include families in the bargain. That means spending more, of course, but it also means a system that's more family-friendly, more conducive to having kids, more hospitable to obtaining new skills—in short, more supportive of a large, productive workforce that will lessen the strain on programs for the aged. It also means a system much less imperiled by the demographic shifts that have placed Medicare and Social Security in danger.

Perhaps the most promising idea for creating such a system is a simple proposal I call "universal insurance"—a kind of umbrella insurance policy protecting families against catastrophic drops in income or budget-wrecking expenses. Premiums would be a small share of total income and payouts would be based on the decline of disposable income from its previous base, with the share of income replaced higher for lower-income families.

Managing Risk

Universal insurance could, in turn, be coupled with a less regressive and dangerous form of personal accounts than those advocated by Bush. These tax-free accounts would help families manage unavoidable household expenses before they reached catastrophic levels. Each year—and upon the birth of children—the government would contribute small amounts to each account. These public contributions would vary inversely with income, offsetting the regressive distribution of the tax breaks.

Universal insurance would protect Americans before they fell into poverty, lessening the burden on programs for the poor and protecting the dignity of beneficiaries. From the standpoint of income protection, what matters is not whether some are rich and others are poor, but whether all Americans are protected against precipitous drops in their standards of living. Universal insurance would depart from existing social insurance programs in providing general risk protection. Its premise would be that Americans need access to more than existing, highly segmented programs—programs that not only leave glaring gaps, but also lack the ability to respond to a rapidly changing world of risk.

To be sure, a risk-centered economic agenda has, well, risks. For one thing, it's sure to be attacked as tax-and-spend liberalism run amok. But, against the cost, one must balance the savings. Billions in hidden taxes are currently imposed by laws that facilitate bankruptcy, mandate emergency room care, and bail out the politically sympathetic when things go bad. And our current system imposes a huge economic drain when people don't change jobs, don't have kids, or don't invest in new skills because they fear the risks of those choices.

The most powerful criticism of a risk-centered agenda, then, will be the same one the right has been trotting out for years: Risk is good. It creates incentives to work hard and climb the economic ladder. Meanwhile, protecting people against risk is bad. It creates what economists call "moral hazard," a reason to take risks we'd otherwise avoid. If government helps people deal with income losses or family crises, it will just encourage more of what it is trying to prevent.

To some extent, this is true—and that's the whole point. Corporations enjoy limited liability precisely to encourage risk-taking. As David Moss argues in his provocative book *When All Else Fails: Government as the Ultimate Risk Manager*, the state has been managing risk since the dawn of the republic, gradually extending the reach of insurance from corporations and the affluent to all Americans. Today, however, the circle of protection is shrinking rather than expanding. We still have limited liability for American corporations, but, increasingly, we have full liability for American families.

Conservatives like Bush are right that the dynamism of the U.S. economy generates huge rewards and that trying to eliminate that dynamism through regulation or protectionism would reduce those rewards. Yet, if we acquiesce to the "creative destruction" of American-style capitalism, then we also have to accept that many Americans, at one point or another, will be hit by disasters with which they cannot cope on their own. Conservatives say free markets create more winners than losers. They say helping the losers is a better way of addressing insecurity than restricting the freedom that begets it. It's time voters demand that they put their money where their mouths are.

6

Income Inequality Obstructs Social and Economic Mobility

Charles R. Morris

Charles R. Morris is the author of American Catholic *and* Money, Greed, and Risk.

In America wealth is concentrated in the hands of a small few. This wealth concentration is the result of inflated executive salaries and tax policies that favor the rich. Wealth concentration discourages social mobility and equal opportunity. The children of the poor now tend to stay poor while the children of the rich tend to stay rich because of tax and fiscal policies that favor the very wealthy. For example, the payroll tax is highly regressive: Middle-class and poorer families pay a larger share of their paychecks in taxes than do those in the upper income brackets. Instead of promoting social policies to promote equal opportunity, the government has promoted policies favorable to the rich, thus accelerating the economic gap between the rich and the poor.

America has always had an ambivalent attitude toward equality. In contrast to the social democratic regimes of Europe, the only officially endorsed equality Americans have historically embraced is the narrow sense of equality of opportunity—as opposed to outcome. A suspicion of government interference in economic matters is an attitude that dates from the early days of the republic. When [French writer Alexis] de Toqueville lauded the rough equality of Americans in the 1830s, he made it clear

Charles R. Morris, "Economic Injustice for Most," *Commonweal*, vol. 131, August 13, 2004, pp. 12–15. Copyright © 2004 by Commonweal Publishing Co., Inc. Reproduced by permission.

that it is the fluidity of the society that impressed him: "I do not mean that there is any lack of wealthy individuals in the United States. . . . But wealth circulates with inconceivable rapidity, and experience shows that it is rare to find two succeeding generations in the full enjoyment of it."

[Abraham] Lincoln made much the same point: "[It is] best to leave each man free to acquire property as fast as he can. Some will get wealthy; I don't believe in a law to prevent a man from getting rich [but] . . . we do wish to allow the humblest man an equal chance to get rich with everyone else." Yet the vast accretions of personal fortunes and corporate power that accompanied the rough-and-tumble era of free-booting capitalism in the decades after the Civil War—when men like [wealthy industrialists] John D. Rockefeller, Andrew Carnegie, and Jay Gould were building their empires—cast doubt on the reality of the American mythos of equal opportunity.

Carnegie loved to pose as the friend of the workingman, basking in the attendant public applause, until the searing events of the 1892 Homestead strike exposed the savage working conditions at his plants—twelve-hour days, seven-day weeks, a single scheduled day off a year, squalid little company towns, contaminated water, near-starvation wages. (After the strike was broken with much violence, Carnegie salved his conscience and burnished his image by giving the borough of Homestead a library.)

> *The current patterns of income concentration are violently out of whack with historical experience, and may indeed be without precedent.*

By 1890, at the height of the Gilded Age, just 1 percent of the population owned slightly more than a quarter of all the nation's wealth. That data was reconstructed by historians, but widespread awareness of a growing, and possibly unbridgeable, chasm between the Haves and the Have-Nots fueled the Populist movement in the last years of the nineteenth century, the Progressive politics and trust-busting initiatives early in the twentieth, and Franklin Roosevelt's New Deal [Depression-era programs]. After World War II, and through the 1950s and 1960s, there was substantial leveling of wealth and income.

The rich were still very rich, but programs like the G.I. Bill [which provides many benefits to World War II veterans] restored the conviction that the ladder Americans had to climb to attain real wealth evidenced the scale of the opportunity rather than the height of the barriers.

Virtually all those gains have been dissipated over the past twenty-five years or so. Instead of controlling a quarter of the nation's wealth, as in the Gilded Age, the richest 1 percent of the population now owns about a third, and the top 5 percent about 58 percent, of all wealth. Those numbers represent the densest concentration of wealth since the peak of American wealth inequality, which was in 1929, a not entirely reassuring precedent.

Income Concentration

The recent trends in income concentration have been even more pronounced than those in wealth. This is unusual and especially worrisome. Wealth accumulations occur over extended periods, so it can take a number of years for even highly skewed income patterns to be fully reflected in wealth distributions. The current patterns of income concentration are violently out of whack with historical experience, and may indeed be without precedent. . . .

Over the thirty years from 1970 to 2000, the bottom 90 percent of earners as a group actually lost ground. All the top 10 percent did well, but only the top 1 percent did extremely well, and even within the top 1 percent gains were disproportionately concentrated within the top hundredth of 1 percent, a mere 13,400 households.

If you read the financial news, you know that the period from 1980 through 2001 marked one of the greatest of American economic booms—when we recovered our competitive position in the world, and created entirely new high-technology industries. Well, guess who reaped all the gains from that hard work? . . . Almost all the benefits flowed to the very rich. The poor, the lower-middle class, the middle class, even the upper-middle class, got almost nothing at all. So much for fairy tales about rising tides.

Special Treatment

The truth is that the amazing spurt in top-drawer incomes is so sudden, so striking, so out of keeping with experiences, that it will take economists years to reach a consensus on the details of what happened, if they ever do. But there are some obvious factors at work.

> *The truth is that the amazing spurt in top-drawer incomes is so sudden, so striking, so out of keeping with experiences, that it will take economists years to reach a consensus on the details of what happened, if they ever do.*

The 1986 Tax Reform Act[1] was a signal nonpartisan accomplishment, worked out between the Reagan administration and a substantially Democratic tax-reform wing of the Congress, led notably by Senator Bill Bradley. The core principle of the reform was to trade a greatly simplified tax code, eliminating almost all special privileges and shelters, for an extraordinary, across-the-board reduction in tax rates and the number of brackets. As far as possible, all income was to be treated alike; there was to be no difference in the taxation of capital gains and ordinary income, no difference between the rentier and the ordinary wage earner. Although the act was sometimes blamed for the era's large deficits, an IRS [Internal Revenue Service] analysis showed that tax receipts actually increased the year after its passage.

Sadly, almost as soon as it was passed, tax advocates for the wealthy began lobbying for a restoration of special tax breaks, especially in the treatment of capital gains. (Taxable capital gains, of course, accrue almost entirely to the wealthy. The current tax exclusion for capital gains on the sale of a home—$500,000 for a couple—effectively eliminates taxes on the vast majority of home sales, while the stocks and bonds owned by ordinary people are mostly in pension funds and 401[k] plans, which are already tax-protected.) By the time the capital gains tax preference was finally restored, in complicated horse-trading with an embattled Clinton administration in 1998, most of the other shelters that benefit the very rich had wormed their way back into the code also. Although there were

1. The Tax Reform Act of 1986, initiated by President Ronald Reagan, eliminated special treatment in capital gains, limited tax shelters, and decreased corporate tax rates.

modest increases in the top rates under the first President Bush and President Bill Clinton, actual tax rates paid by top-tier earners stayed flat or fell, even as their incomes steadily rose.

A second factor was a devastating campaign of vilification against the Internal Revenue Service by the Newt Gingrich wing of the Republican Party. A thoroughly cowed agency drastically reduced its auditing activities to the point where the working poor—who can receive a maximum $4,120 benefit under the Earned Income Tax Credit—were more likely to be audited than substantial small businesses, and three times more likely than individuals earning more than $100,000. By all reports tax evasion has soared, as evidenced by the aggressive marketing of illegal tax shelters by some of our most august financial institutions.

There was also an extraordinary outbreak of greed on the part of Wall Street executives and business leaders. By 1999, the average pay of the 100 top CEOs [chief executive officers] was $37 million. Between 1970 and 2000, the average American worker's paycheck improved by about $2 a week each year, mostly resulting from gains made by women. At the same time, CEO pay improved $26,000 a week each year—every year for thirty years. The almost inconceivable leap in executive income has naturally stimulated a free-for-all rush for even more tax privileges and shelters—special treatment for stock options, offshore hedge funds, companies paying for personal expenses, tax benefits for owning corporate jets, and many, many more. That such unseemly looting has become socially acceptable, not to say praiseworthy, is an inquiry for social psychology, not economics.

> **" By the standards of other developed countries, Social Security is modest enough, yet it is still the most important . . . antipoverty program. "**

Finally, it is worth noting that virtually all these data are from the period before the recent Bush administration tax cuts on capital gains, stock dividends, and estate taxes. Taken together, the Bush program will beam the very rich out to new galaxies of wealth far, far, away from the rest of us. The single-mindedness with which the administration has focused on benefits for the narrow band of the super-rich is astonishing. Congressional Democrats, for example, have proposed raising the ceiling on the estate tax to $4 million, or a similarly high figure, rather than totally eliminating it. The administration responds with ritual denunciations of "death taxes" on "small businesses" and "family farmers." In fact, the most recent data on average estates at death show that for people in the 99–99.5th percentile of income, the average estate was only about $2.1 million. The big winners from the Bush program are our 13,400 friends in the top .01 percent whose average estate was about $87 million. This is a tax platform that would make Louis XIV [king of France, 1638–1715] proud.

Declining Mobility

The problem is not that some people are getting rich. Lincoln was right that the fluidity and mobility of America make up a great part of its attraction. But there are many problems with developing a class of super-rich. For one thing, as the tiering of American wealth distribution stretches further and further upward, it reduces mobility. The children of the poor now disproportionately stay poor, to an extent far beyond any explication based on lower intelligence or race, while the children of the rich disproportionately stay rich, again to an extent that can't be explained by their talent or IQs. There is also substantial evidence that a number of other developed countries—including Germany, Canada, Sweden, and Finland—now have more social mobility than America does. The justification for policies that mildly even out wealth accumulation is much like those for regulating business competition. Americans are in favor of free competition and applaud the winners, but we also believe that it is right to step in to level the playing field when competition ends in monopoly.

Then there is the problem of corruption, as illustrated by the naked bias of the current administration toward its friends among the very wealthy. *New York Times* reporter David Cay Johnston, in his fine recent book, *Perfectly Legal* (Portfolio/Penguin), has documented case after case where the administration or its congressional friends have engineered egregious giveaways to tiny coteries of the very wealthiest people in America.

These are not just theoretical problems. An obvious example of how pandering to the very wealthiest is destructive of the interests of everyone else is the administration's insistence on outlawing Medicare from negotiating better pharmaceutical prices for its enrollees. Even more important is the current attack on Social Security. It's a complex story but worth tracing in some detail.

By the standards of other developed countries, Social Security is modest enough, yet it is still the most important American antipoverty program. About 45 million people receive benefits from the program. More than a third of beneficiaries are disabled, or are the children and spouses of disabled or retired workers. For more than two-thirds of retirees, Social Security is more than half their income. In 1983, on the recommendations of a commission chaired by Alan Greenspan, who was then not in government, Congress passed a thorough overhaul of the system's financing. There was a very sharp increase in payroll taxes for Social Security and Medicare, the age for full retirement was pushed up on a phased basis, and certain benefits were subject to taxation. The payroll tax increase was much larger than needed to support current Social Security outlays. The extra payments were designed to build an interest-earning surplus in the Social Security trust funds to provide a cushion against the day, now almost upon us, when the baby boomers begin to retire in large numbers.

The payroll tax itself is unusually regressive. It falls on the first dollar of income up to a ceiling . . . ; upper-income people are consequently assessed a lower share of their paychecks than average workers are. For most middle-class and poorer families, the payroll tax is the largest tax they pay, and substantially reduces the overall progressivity of federal taxes. (On a lifetime basis, the effect of Social Security taxes and benefits is still mildly progressive for most people.)

Economic Crises

The Bush administration has been loudly proclaiming that Social Security is in terminal crisis. The truth, according to the best current projections, is that assets of the Social Security trust funds will be sufficient to cover benefits for the next thirty-eight years. Additional tweaks will be required to ensure solvency beyond that; but if they're enacted now, they can be relatively mild. Some combination of a 1-percent or so payroll-tax increase together with a modest slowdown in the rate of benefit increases, or a variety of similar measures, would about do the trick. So why is the administration shouting crisis? Because they want to "privatize" the system—that is, take the accumulated trillions of dollars in the trust funds and give them to their friends on Wall Street to manage (yes, the same folks who brought us the dot.com fiasco). A 1-percent management fee on a trillion dollars is $10 billion a year, so we're not talking about chump change. In fact, for complicated reasons, privatization will actually make the system's financing much worse, but the administration simply ignores that. After all, that's what friends are for.

But the Bush tax and fiscal policies will be even more devastating for Social Security than privatization would be. The Bush tax cuts are aimed at virtually eliminating taxes on investment income—especially capital gains, corporate dividends, and accumulated estates—all of which will serve to increase the yawning gap between the very rich and everyone else. Although the administration originally sold the tax cuts as a temporary expedient to restore growth, it is now pressing to make them permanent. The consequence will be very large federal deficits, of a scale not seen since the worst deficits of the Reagan years. Although administration flacks blame the deficits on slow growth, the nonpartisan Congressional Budget Office identifies the tax cuts as the largest single factor.

Why will deficits do so much damage? Follow what happens to those payroll tax surpluses. The government takes in the cash and spends it for general government purposes like the war in Iraq, subsidies for sugar beet farmers, and Medicare. Then the government issues an interest-bearing bond in the same amount and deposits it in the Social Security trust funds. One level of government—the Social Security administration— now owns a bond, and another level of the same government has the obligation to pay it off when it falls due.

At some point, in about fifteen years or so, payroll taxes will no longer cover annual retirement payments. At that point, the trust funds will begin to cash in their bonds. Where will the government get the cash to pay them off? There are only two ways—it can raise taxes or borrow. The original idea behind the payroll tax surpluses was that they would help the government pay down its accumulated debt, so it would have plenty of borrowing power when the boomer bills start to fall due. That was actually happening at a rapid clip during the second Clinton administration.

But if the government just keeps adding to its debt by running massive budget deficits, it won't have any extra borrowing power to manage Social Security payments, and there will also be many more claims on potential tax increases. That leaves only two expedients—just print lots of new money, and inflate away the value of the benefits; or renege on Social Security's promises.

Federal Reserve Chairman Alan Greenspan understands the conflict between the Bush deficits and the promises of Social Security. That is why he issued a statement earlier this year calling for major cuts in benefits. Yes, this is the same Alan Greenspan who has consistently supported the Bush tax cuts, and who also strongly supports making them permanent, thus locking in the deficits. It is also the same Alan Greenspan who favors turning over the trust funds to Wall Street investment bankers—so they can get even more amazingly rich than normal people. And yes, this is the same Alan Greenspan who designed the current Social Security financing system in the first place.

In short, twenty years of the high payroll taxes Greenspan recommended to finance Social Security have been blown away by a binge of upper-class tax cuts, which Greenspan also advocated. So now your benefits will have to be cut to make up the difference. You trusted the government with your payroll tax surplus, and were proved a sucker. The fees Greenspan and the administration would like to take from the trust funds for their friends on Wall Street are just another bonus.

It would be hard to imagine a more naked case of aggression by the wealthiest on the interests of the rest of the citizenry. There is only one word for it—it is a crime.

7

Income Inequality Does Not Lead to Greater Poverty

Jonah Goldberg

Jonah Goldberg is the editor of National Review Online.

Some people argue that growing economic inequality leads to greater poverty. In fact, the poor do not fall further into poverty because wealthy individuals have doubled or tripled their wealth, and wealthy people do not prevent the poor from advancing economically. On the contrary, when wealthy people become wealthier, they provide more opportunities for other people to also advance. In addition, poverty is relative; many people who would be considered poor by American standards would seem positively rich compared to someone living in a third-world nation. The typical "poor" American as defined by the U.S. Census Bureau owns a car, air conditioning, a VCR, and a color TV. Furthermore, child hunger has largely been eliminated in the United States.

If [cofounder and chairman of Microsoft] Bill Gates and I started our own country in which we were the only residents—call it Gatesbergia—it would be wracked by the worst income inequality in the world. The "haves" of the society would make hundreds of thousands of times more money than the "have nots." The disparities of wealth in our nation would be worse than those in Brazil, Nigeria or even—gasp—the United States. And, if Warren Buffet, the Sultan of Brunei and Rupert

Jonah Goldberg, "Rich-Poor Divide Shows Poverty Is Relative," www.townhall.com, June 18, 2003. Copyright © 2003 by Tribune Media Services. Reproduced by permission.

Murdoch immigrated to Gatesbergia, the problem would be even worse, for the gap would get wider and I would be "left behind."

Now, even though the rich-poor disparity of Gatesbergia would be "bad," I would not be in bad shape. In fact, I could live quite well in Gatesbergia, even though what I make every year is less than a rounding error on Bill Gates' tax return.

> **"** *The typical 'poor' American, according to census data has a car, air conditioning, a refrigerator, a stove, a VCR and a color TV.* **"**

Indeed, I could prosper. After all, Bill Gates and the sultan would surely pay me very well to clean their houses, cook their food and tie their shoes. Soon I could become a millionaire, even as the low taxes and pro-business policies of Gatesbergia sent the billionaires even further and faster into the income stratosphere. So, in effect, even as the rich-poor gap got wider, I'd get richer.

I offer this illustration because we're poised to enter another round of hand-wringing over income inequality in America. The editorials and op-eds on the subject are multiplying and intensifying. . . .

Poverty Is Relative

Now, the first thing to keep fresh in your mind is that high income inequality is not the same thing as high poverty. As the Gatesbergia example illustrates, you can have outrageous gaps between the rich and poor and the "poor" will still be OK.

For example, according to Robert Rector, an economist with the Heritage Foundation who uses the government's numbers, the typical person in the poorest fifth of U.S. households today spends as much as the person of average wealth in the early 1970s (adjusted for inflation).

The typical "poor" American, according to census data has a car, air conditioning, a refrigerator, a stove, a VCR and a color TV. It should go without saying—but usually doesn't—that in, say, 1960, someone who had a color TV, a refrigerator, air conditioning and a car would not be considered poor.

More telling: Child hunger has largely been wiped out as a

major social problem in America. While deplorable instances of hungry children still occur (usually attributable to bad parenting), the real nutritional problem we face today is fat kids.

Not only is poverty relative, it has less to do with money than most people think. Technological innovation makes life less expensive. Fifty years ago, a refrigerator was a big investment, even for the middle class. But it was worth it because it made it possible to buy food in bulk.

Today, refrigerators may not be supercheap, but they're affordable. And the cheapest fridge today is far more advanced than a fridge from two decades ago. Ten years ago, a cell phone was a luxury. Today, they're ubiquitous—even in the poorest neighborhoods.

Here's how relative our understanding of poverty is: The average poor person in America is richer than many entire villages in Africa or Asia, where they still have no phones, refrigerators, and very little food.

Income Inequality and Poverty

Many on the left—particularly those still in a Marxist haze—reject the idea that poverty should be viewed in absolute terms. But when you think about it, they have to. If we all agreed that many of the poorest people in America live with the material prosperity—cars, phones, air conditioning, the caloric intake of a Roman emperor—we associated with millionaires just a few generations ago, most of the liberal agenda would have to go out the window.

Of course, this is all easy for me to say. I don't live in poverty, relative or absolute. And many millions of people are struggling to make ends meet, put food on the table and educate their kids. But that's not because of income inequality. If Bill Gates doubled his income tomorrow, poor people would still have a hard time. Income inequality doesn't make people poor, it just strikes some people as unfair.

But some economists believe that if Bill Gates and those like him got a lot richer, there'd be fewer poor people. In a new book put out by the American Enterprise Institute, *Inequality and Tax Policy*, contributor Robert Barro of Harvard notes that in wealthy countries, there's a strong link between rising income inequality and rising economic growth.

That's the way you'd think it would work, in Gatesbergia and in America.

8

Income Inequality Benefits American Society

Christopher J. Coyne

Christopher J. Coyne is a PhD candidate in economics and a James M. Buchanan Fellow at George Mason University in Fairfax, Virginia.

In a free market, capitalist society, all individuals are considered equal before the law, and no one is legally bound to any particular caste or economic class. Individuals are thus free to compete and advance to an elevated economic status. It is this mobility and fluidity that make the American economy dynamic and innovative. Any attempts to achieve an egalitarian society by redistributing income destroy the individuality and freedom that are crucial to the development of society. If people are not allowed to keep the fruits of their labor, they lose the motivation to innovate and specialize and create the goods that benefit the economy and society. It is therefore dangerous and counterproductive to try to guarantee the same income to everyone.

In a recent article, Paul Krugman [a *New York Times* columnist] pines for the lost America of the 1950s and 1960s, which he characterizes as a "middle class society". While inequality existed, Krugman tells us, it was not nearly as bad as the [nineteenth-century] Gilded Age where robber barons ran roughshod over the less fortunate. It is Krugman's contention that the United States has returned to a Gilded Age as extravagant as the original, characterized by the widening gap between the haves and have nots.

While pointing out the many social and economic "problems" in the U.S., Krugman fails to offer any recommendations regarding how to fix them. Here, I would like to focus on two issues that are the foundation of Krugman's analysis. They are (1) the idea of class distinction, or class struggle, which leads to (2) the notion of inequality as bad and equality as good. These concepts are not exclusive to Krugman—we hear them used on a daily basis by politicians, the media and economists among others. It makes sense then to explore them in more detail.

Throughout the article, Krugman warns that he will be accused of "class warfare" for focusing on the topic of inequality. While we will not fault him for this, we do find fault in his incorrect characterization of class distinction as a struggle between static groups. Simply put, Krugman obfuscates the problem of inequality by confusing the notions of class and caste. In a caste society, individuals inherit their caste membership from their parents. Only in exceptional cases can a man rise to a higher caste; birth determines his position in life. As [Austrian economist Ludwig von] Mises, writing on [Communist icon Karl] Marx and his theories, indicates:

> Where status and caste differences prevail, all members of every caste but the most privileged have one interest in common, viz., to wipe out the legal disabilities of their own caste. All slaves for instance, are united in having a stake in the abolition of slavery. But no such conflicts are present in a society in which all citizens are equal before the law. No logical objection can be advanced distinguishing various classes among the members of such a society.

Social Mobility

In a capitalist society, no such distinction of classes as castes can be made. Any distinction of classes only serves to represent some snapshot in time as movement between classes is continually fluctuating. This is in stark contrast to the caste system where affiliation with a class or caste is hereditary and largely unchanging. Turning again to Mises:

> It [class membership in a capitalist society] is as-

signed to each individual by a daily repeated plebiscite, as it were, of all the people. The public in spending and buying determines who should own and run the plants, who should play the parts in the theater performances, who should work in the factories and mines. Rich men become poor, and poor men rich. The heirs as well as those who themselves have acquired wealth must try to hold their own by defending their assets against the competition of already established firms and of ambitious newcomers.

The market provides no privileges and does not discriminate based on sex, religion, income, etc. Individuals are free to move between classes based on their ability to satiate the desires of others. All agents, regardless of class are in competition with *all* other members of society. Assuming that all individuals are equal before the law, all are free to compete for any and all social positions as they wish. All that stands in their way is their natural abilities and their ambition to serve the needs of others.

> *Individuals are free to move between classes based on their ability to satiate the desires of others.*

This leads us directly to the notion of inequality. Only by freezing individual incomes at some moment in time are we able to consider class distinctions. Having established these clear-cut classes, one is then able to see that some have more relative to others. That is, they are unequal.

Initially, we must ask, why is equality the social goal toward which we strive? This is a broad ethical goal which Krugman completely fails to justify. Is our end goal a state of the world where all individuals have exactly equal incomes? Is there some degree of inequality (i.e., an "income gap") that is acceptable? If so, why? If not, why not? These questions aside, let us further consider the notion of equality. [Political writer Murray N.] Rothbard provides a clear explanation:

> Let us take three entities: *A, B* and *C. A, B,* and *C* are said to be 'equal' to each other (i.e., A=B=C) *if*

a particular characteristic is found in which the three entities are uniform or identical. It follows that A, B, and C can be completely 'equal' to each other only if they are identical or uniform in all characteristics. We see, then, that the ideal of human equality *can only* imply total uniformity and the utter stamping out of individuality.

Attempts at imposed equality destroy individuality. Individuality allows for specialization, the division of labor and economic progress. When it is hampered, so are these outgrowths. The critic may vociferously object: "Krugman is only calling for equality of income, not equality in all areas of life!" Our response is that the two are inextricably related.

Individuality and Progress

Freedom is central to individual progress and hence the development of society as a whole. Allowing individuals to keep the fruits of their labor is a critical part of this freedom. Coercively extracting any part of his income directly violates this freedom. Any attempt to achieve equality is an attempt to erode, and ultimately destroy, individuality. From this perspective, calling for equality of incomes is the first step toward destroying individuality and attempting to transform men into homogeneous automatons, devoid of any unique and specific traits. Of course, the one exception is equality before the law since this allows man to develop his unique abilities and talents which in turn leads to economic progress.

Let us return to our discussion of equal income. If all are guaranteed the same income, the result will be twofold. First, there will be widespread government intervention in attempts to redistribute wealth to those who are determined to be "unequal". Second, the incentive for investment, specialization, creativity and entrepreneurship will be destroyed. Krugman rejects the latter claim by arguing that U.S. productivity in the 1990s was no better as compared to the great postwar expansion.

Hence he concludes that incentives are not as powerful as one would think. Intuitively, this seems peculiar. If all individuals are making exactly the same income no matter what their effort, what would be man's motivation to act? Would man's very nature transform so that he would become stronger, wiser, and more harmonious? Would he rise to the level of [Greek philosopher] Aristotle or Marx as [Soviet Communist revolutionary Leon] Trotsky predicted? Krugman fails to provide the reader with a definite answer.

Incorrect ideas must be identified and their errors must be corrected. Dangerous ideas must be destroyed. The notions of class distinction and equality no doubt fall into the latter category. For these ideas stand counter to the foundational underpinnings of freedom, individuality and economic progress. Only when these ideas are thoroughly eradicated and markets truly embraced will we realize the true potential of mankind as unique and unequal individuals.

9

Personal Choices Increase the Gap Between the Rich and Poor

Isabel V. Sawhill

Isabel V. Sawhill is a senior fellow, director of economic studies, and vice president of the Brookings Institution, a nonpartisan Washington think tank.

The wealthy and the poor exhibit different behavioral patterns. The rich have embraced traditional patterns of behavior, such as getting married, gaining an education, and obtaining steady employment. The poor, on the other hand, have largely abandoned these patterns of behavior that contribute to upward mobility. These differences in behavior have accelerated the growing economic inequality between the rich and the poor. The government should offer incentives such as tax credits that will promote marriage and employment and thereby alleviate the problems faced by the underclass.

In a famous exchange between [Ernest] Hemingway and [F. Scott] Fitzgerald, Fitzgerald is reputed to have said, "The rich are different from the rest of us," to which Hemingway replied, "Yes, I know, they have more money." Liberals have long contended that Hemingway had it right. There is nothing wrong with the poor that a little more money wouldn't cure. This view is, I believe, profoundly misguided. Money can alleviate

Isabel V. Sawhill, "The Behavioral Aspects of Poverty," *Public Interest*, Fall 2003, pp. 79–95.

the harsh conditions of poverty, but unless it is used to lever-
age changes in behavior, it will have little lasting effect.

Not only does behavior matter, it matters more than it used
to. Growing gaps between rich and poor in recent decades have
been exacerbated by a divergence in the behavior of the two
groups. No feasible amount or income redistribution can make
up for the fact that the rich are working and marrying as much
or more than ever while the poor are doing just the reverse.
Unless the poor adopt more mainstream behaviors, and public
policies are designed to move them in this direction, economic
divisions are likely to grow.

A Tale of Two Families

In the 1990s, two journalists independently chronicled the
lives of two inner-city families in Washington, D.C. Both journalists would eventually win Pulitzer Prizes for their reporting,
but the portraits they painted could not have been more different. One of them, Leon Dash, a reporter with the *Washington
Post*, followed the life history of Rosa Lee Cunningham and her
family. At the time, Cunningham was a 52-year-old grandmother who had had her first child at age 14 and dropped out
of school. The daughter of North Carolina sharecroppers, she
grew up near Capitol Hill, and then supported herself by wait-
ing tables, working as a prostitute, selling drugs, and shoplift-
ing. She became addicted to heroin and spent time in prison
for drug trafficking. She had eight children fathered by six different men and all but two of them became, like their mother,
involved in drugs, crime, and teenage parenting.

> *Growing gaps between rich and poor in recent
> decades have been exacerbated by a divergence in
> the behavior of the two groups.*

Contrast this with another story of the inner city, told by
Ron Suskind, a reporter with the *Wall Street Journal*. Suskind followed the life of a teenager named Cedric Jennings, who at the
time lived with his mother in the same kind of inner-city
neighborhood as Cunningham. But Cedric's mother, Barbara,
had three children and had worked for 11 years at a five-dollar-

an-hour job as a data-input clerk for the Department of Agriculture. She attended church regularly, lived frugally, supervised her children closely, and had instilled in her son a fierce desire to succeed. Cedric not only became an honor student at Ballou High School but eventually gained admittance to Brown University.

As these stories suggest, people living in poverty are a diverse group. Some are poor primarily because, like Cunningham, they persist in perverse and antisocial behavior. Others, like Jennings, have done the best they can with limited resources. Thus the two contending views of what causes poverty—people's own behavior or their adverse circumstances—will have some validity at least some of the time. Most poor people are neither as down and out as Cunningham nor as hard-working and dedicated to their children's success as Jennings. But what more systematic research shows is that behavior matters and must be taken into account if we are to reduce poverty and inequality.

Ideology vs. Reality

My own involvement in this debate began in the late 1980s, when the Rockefeller Foundation established a program of research on what it called "the underclass." The underclass was commonly defined as those families living in areas of concentrated poverty, usually in neighborhoods where at least 40 percent of all households were poor. At the time, I was a scholar at the Urban Institute, a Washington think tank, and I suggested an alternative definition, one that was more behaviorally oriented. It was based on the idea that in order to achieve a middle-class life, an individual must do a few specific things: graduate from high school, defer having a baby until marriage, and obtain steady employment. With the help of several colleagues, I estimated the number of people who lived in neighborhoods where the basic norms of middle-class life had eroded to the point where a large fraction of residents had failed to do these three things. Our research showed that the underclass, thus defined, was still quite small, heavily concentrated in large urban areas, disproportionately made up of racial minorities, and, at the time, growing. I was especially concerned about the prospects of the children growing up in these environments where few men were working, most women were unmarried and on welfare, and dropping out of school was commonplace. Not only were most of the children in these neighborhoods living in poverty, but they lacked the kind of role models that would enable them to take advantage of the opportunities that did exist.

> **"Poverty in America is overwhelmingly associated with the failure to work on a full-time basis."**

The reactions to this study were as interesting as the findings themselves. Some people, including Dash and Suskind, embraced my research for providing the kind of big picture in which their own stories could be embedded. A much more common reaction from scholars, however, was to suggest that talking about the culture of the underclass was tantamount to "blaming the victim." Bad behavior and poor choices, in this view, were an understandable adaptation to poverty and the lack of opportunity in people's lives. Although my research on the underclass was given a polite reception, most of the academic community has coalesced around the view that bad behaviors are a consequence, rather than a cause, of poverty. The result was that scholars continued to define the underclass simply in economic terms.

The reason for this reaction has more to do, I think, with ideology than with reality. Most academics, myself included, feel considerable sympathy for those who are poor or disadvantaged. We understand that none of us is perfect; and that while bad habits and poor discipline are widespread, they are more consequential for those living on the margin, where any slip-up may tumble someone over the edge. Moreover, children's starting points are very uneven. As a result liberals are wary of taking a judgmental stance, and fear that by "blaming the victim" they will undercut the political will to provide more resources to the poor. The problem with this mindset is that it requires avoiding or downplaying some unpleasant facts. . . .

The Importance of Work

What areas of behavior are we talking about? As I have suggested, three are critical. The first is education; the second is family formation; and the third is work. These have always been the sources of upward mobility in advanced democracies.

Those who graduate from high school, wait until marriage to have children, limit the size of their families, and work full-time will not be poor.

This last statement may be surprising, but it is true. Every year the Census Bureau collects detailed information on a large and representative sample of all households in the United States. From these data, the government calculates the poverty rate for all households. In the year 2001, 12 percent of all households were found to live in poverty. The government's official poverty line in that year was $9,214 for a single individual living alone and $17,960 for a family of four. However, the poverty rate for those households where the primary wage-earner had finished high school, was married, had no more than two children, and worked full-time (2,000 hours a year or more) was trivially small—1 percent.

> **//** With the availability of birth control and legal abortions having made unplanned parenthood unnecessary, it is hard to understand why so many women are having babies that they cannot support. **//**

Of these three things, the most important is full-time work. To understand the importance of work alone in reducing poverty, perform the following thought-experiment. First take every family where there is at least one adult who is not too old or sick to work. Next assume that that adult is employed full-time at a wage commensurate with his or her education and experience. Under this assumption, almost half of those who are currently below the government's official poverty line would not be poor. The poverty rate would fall by a full five percentage points. Contrast this scenario with another, in which we double the amount of welfare benefits provided to America's poor. One might imagine that this would make them far better off. In fact, it does not. It reduces the poverty rate by only one percentage point.

Poverty in America is overwhelmingly associated with the failure to work on a full-time basis. Many immigrant families do well in the United States despite their lack of education because they tend to form stable families and work harder than many similarly disadvantaged native-born Americans. Yet these mobility-enhancing behaviors, and the attitudes that foster them, often disappear within a generation or two, suggesting that it may be aspects of American culture rather than economic stresses alone that hinder further progress. The more general conclusion is that attitudes and behavior matter. If you stay in school, work hard, marry, and have a reasonable number of children, you may still struggle financially, but you will certainly not be destitute.

Choice or Opportunity?

This general conclusion is undermined, of course, to the extent that these behaviors are less a matter of choice than of opportunity. Not all parents encourage their children to do well in school; some adults can't find steady jobs; and some men and women have difficulty finding people to marry or end up in troubled marriages through no fault of their own. Even efforts to limit the size of one's family may fail—although repeated failures that lead to a much larger family than one can support are hard to excuse, since birth control is now widely available and highly effective.

The problem is that there are many gray areas where it's difficult to discern what circumstances are chosen and which are the result of a lack of opportunity. Take the issue of work. Liberals contend that people are unemployed or work too few hours because work isn't available. The fact that employment rates among the least skilled rise when overall economic conditions improve suggests that there is some merit to this argument. Yet the much more limited work effort on the part of the poor persists in good times as well as bad. Moreover, surveys of the jobless suggest that a lack of jobs is not the primary reason for their failure to find and maintain employment. In 1999, when the Census Bureau interviewed the heads of poor families about their failure to work in the preceding year, only 6 percent of women and 12 percent of men said they were unable to find work. The remainder cited reasons such as their obligations to school, job training, and family for their lack of employment. Clearly, many of the jobs available to those with limited education are low-paying and disagreeable. For these reasons, and because they often have access to other sources of income such as welfare, illegal earnings, or help from relatives, many of the unemployed are not interested in taking these jobs. Still others are depressed, addicted, or have prison records that make regular employment difficult if not impossible. Providing these hard-to-employ individuals with a welfare or disability check may be better than leaving them homeless, especially if they have children. But such cash assistance does not address their more basic behavioral problems. One unintended consequence of the tough welfare law enacted in 1996 is that it has forced welfare offices to grapple with these hard-to-help cases—cases that in the past could be conveniently forgotten once the application had been processed and the welfare check mailed. . . .

Reconsidering Marriage

The Aid to Families with Dependent Children (AFDC) system was created in the 1930s with the explicit purpose of enabling single parents to care for children in their own homes. The assumption was not only that single mothers shouldn't be expected to work, but also that no one becomes a single parent by choice. In those days, most of the women on AFDC were widows, and almost all children were born inside marriage. By the 1990s, this was no longer the case. Most modern-day single mothers on welfare have never been married. They typically have their first baby as a teenager and go onto welfare shortly thereafter. In the meantime, the vast majority of middle-class mothers, including those with young children, now work and pay the taxes that help to support these stay-at-home moms. No wonder welfare is unpopular with the public. President [Bill] Clinton understood this when he pledged to "end welfare as we know it" in 1992. Egged on by Republicans in Congress, he signed the tough welfare-reform bill of 1996. Congress and the Bush administration are now attempting to reauthorize the law, and once again the debate is about whether, or how much, recipients should be required to work and whether resources should be devoted to encouraging marriage.[1]

Many scholars continue to argue that marriage is an unrealistic goal for many of the poor. They point to the lack of employed men in low-income neighborhoods and cite the significant number that are in prison. But they also fail to stress the importance of finishing school and getting a steady job before taking on the responsibility of raising a child. Although a good

1. In 2003 Congress began the process of reauthorizing the historic, bipartisan 1996 Welfare Reform Act, which expired at the end of that year.

job is no substitute for a second parent, it at least ensures that the child will not grow up in poverty. With the availability of birth control and legal abortions having made unplanned parenthood unnecessary, it is hard to understand why so many women are having babies that they cannot support. Many suspect the welfare system has been an enabling factor in these women's bad choices—choices that are further reinforced by the decline in social stigma.

> *The difference in attitudes toward work and marriage between rich and poor have been steadily increasing, with disturbing implications for the children of the poor.*

As evidence of the benefits to children of growing up in a two-parent family has strengthened, liberals have become less likely to question the value of marriage. But many liberals still argue that marriage is no cure for poverty. About this, they are wrong. Adam Thomas, now a doctoral student at Harvard, and I recently conducted a statistical exercise in which we identified all of the single mothers interviewed by the Census Bureau and then matched them up with unmarried men of the same race, education, and age. If enough marriages had taken place to return the incidence of single parenting to 1970 levels, and the incomes of the men and women involved were combined, the poverty rate among children in 1998 would have fallen by about a third. (For certain subgroups of African-American women we did find a shortage of eligible men, some of which may be due to the difficulty the Census Bureau has in locating these men and some of which is due to the large number who have died at a young age or been incarcerated.) . . .

A Behavioral Divide

Policies that support work and marriage are not just an antidote to short-term poverty. They also have a role to play in preventing our country's economic and social divisions from growing even wider. The difference in attitudes toward work and marriage between rich and poor have been steadily increasing, with disturbing implications for the children of the poor.

Consider trends in employment. Historically, the poor have worked long hours to compensate for their lack of skills and low pay, and leisure has been the province of the rich. But, as Gary Burtless at the Brookings Institution has documented, in recent decades people at the bottom of the income distribution have worked fewer hours than those at the top. Since 1968, total hours of work have increased significantly among the entire working-age population, mainly because more women have entered the labor force. But the increases have been largest for those at the top, while the number of hours has actually dropped for those at the bottom. Hours of work increased slightly among men at the top but fell by one-third among adult men in the bottom income quintile. Women's hours increased for both income groups, but the gains were much larger at the top. These changes in hours worked are exacerbating preexisting income gaps between rich and poor. Changes in hourly rates of pay over this period have also favored the more advantaged, but this growing salary gap has been greatly amplified by a growing hours gap.

The story surrounding marriage is similar. Not only are fewer people marrying than in the past, but the trends have affected the haves and have-nots quite differently. Several years ago, I studied the family environments of American children under the age of six. I found that over the past two decades an increasing proportion were being born into a high-risk environment, defined as one in which the child's mother is a high school dropout, is not married, had her first child as a teen, and has a poverty-level income. Most of the children growing up in these circumstances will likely end up repeating the cycle of poverty. Many will do poorly in school, become unwed parents, and will have difficulty supporting themselves as adults. While some children will overcome the odds, their prospects are seriously compromised. . . .

Thinking About the Future

Where does this evidence lead? It suggests we will become even more a divided nation of haves and have-nots unless strong measures are undertaken to change these poverty-inducing behaviors at the bottom and ward off the damage they inflict on the next generation. These measures should not deny assistance to the poor, but should link assistance to a change in behavior.

Policies that are inconsistent with this premise must be discarded. Expanding the Earned Income Tax Credit (EITC), on the other hand, makes enormous sense. The EITC is an income supplement provided to low-income families with working parents. A parent earning $10,000 a year can qualify for as much as $4,000 a year in tax refunds. This is the equivalent of turning a $6-an-hour job into an $8.40-an-hour job. Unlike an increase in the minimum wage, it doesn't affect employers' labor costs and hence their willingness to hire low-skilled workers. And it has a powerful record of encouraging work. Single mothers, the group most affected by recent expansions in the EITC, have moved into the workforce in droves. Their employment rate increased from 57 percent to 74 percent between 1992 and 2000. Unfortunately, the EITC's effects on marriage are not so benign. If a single mother marries another low-wage worker, she will lose most of this benefit. Congress took some steps toward reducing the EITC's marriage penalty in 2001, but more needs to be done. . . .

My purpose is not to recommend any particular program. Rather, it is to stress the importance of aligning policy with what we know about the importance of certain behaviors in reducing poverty and inequality. There is both reason to applaud the steps that have been taken to require and reward work in the 1990s and room for experimentation with bolder measures. Not only will these "tough love" policies be more effective than the cash welfare policies of the past, but they will be more popular with the public. We cannot afford to allow American society to fragment into two cultures, one rich and one poor.

10

Marital Status Separates the Rich from the Poor

Jonathan Rauch

Jonathan Rauch is a senior writer and columnist for the National Journal.

There is a strong correlation between marital status and poverty. Children born into singe-parent households are more likely to be poor than are children born into households with married parents. They are also more likely to experience problems in school, teen pregnancy, and adult unemployment—all of which contribute to a cycle of poverty. Research shows that having married parents is a greater factor than race or income in determining a child's success in life. Given the major disadvantages of single parenthood, government and society need to find ways to promote marriage as a way to reduce poverty.

In the debate over the reauthorization of the landmark 1996 welfare law[1] conservatives are talking about marriage. And talking, and talking. "The conservatives are on an absolute tear about that," says Isabel V. Sawhill, an economist and poverty scholar at the Brookings Institution. "They just never stop talking about it." In March [2001], Rep. Wally Herger, R-Calif., the chairman of the Ways and Means Committee's Human Resources Subcommittee, told this magazine: "During the first phase of welfare reform, we made sure we were putting people

1. The Personal Responsibility and Work Opportunity Reconciliation Act of 1996 replaced the previous welfare program (Temporary Assistance for Needy Families).

to work. I believe that now is the time to stress the importance of marriage."

Liberals and many moderates are reacting to the Right's marriage offensive with understandable wariness. Feminists toward the left end of the spectrum think the government's job is to help single mothers support themselves independently. Mainstream liberals believe that marriage is a good thing and are all for encouraging it, but they doubt that conservatives know how. They worry, reasonably enough, that every federal dollar spent on gestural "pro-marriage" initiatives is one less federal dollar for other anti-poverty and pro-family measures that are more likely to work, such as efforts to prevent teenage pregnancy. Besides, isn't the government getting a bit pushy when it begins pressing people to get hitched?

> *According to Census Bureau data, a two-parent black household is more likely to be poor than is a two-parent white household, but both are far less likely to be poor than is a mother-only household of either race.*

The mainstream liberals have a point. If federal marriage policy works as well as federal agricultural policy, we'll all have a problem. Nonetheless, if the unfolding welfare debate shines a spotlight on marriage, that will be a good thing. The reason is that marriage is displacing both income and race as the great class divide of the new century.

This week's release of fresh data from the 2000 census brought the news that now, for the first time, fewer than a quarter of American households consist of married couples with children, and that, as the *New York Times* reported, the number of single-mother families with children "grew nearly five times faster in the 1990s than the number of married couples with children."

To understand the class implications of that news, begin with a number: 33. That is the percentage of all American children born out of wedlock in 1999, the most recent year for which figures are available. Now another number: 69. That is the percentage of black children born out of wedlock in 1999. The good news is that the illegitimacy ratio for blacks stopped rising in the 1990s; the bad news is that it stabilized at more than triple the illegitimacy ratio of 1960. Today, about two-thirds of all black families are headed by a single parent (usually the mother), and a majority of all black children live in fatherless households.

Ah, you say, yawning: This is just one more manifestation of America's enduring race problem. But is it? Until the 1950s, blacks were more, rather than less, likely than whites to be married. If race is the problem, why did marriage collapse in so much of black America even as Jim Crow [discriminatory laws] and segregation were dismantled and as blacks began entering the economic and social mainstream? And why is the trend similar among whites?

Granted, in white America, marriage and two-parent households are more the rule than the exception. Still, the numbers are sobering. In 1960, about 2 percent of white children were born out of wedlock; in 1999, the comparable figure was 27 percent—and the figure for whites, unlike the one for blacks, continues to grow.

The result is that, by some estimates, 60 percent of all American children born in the 1990s will spend some significant portion of their childhood in a fatherless home. Moreover, the great engine of single-parenthood is no longer divorce, as it was in the 1960s and 1970s; it is the rising share of births to people who never marry to begin with.

Poverty and Marital Status

Some—many—unwed mothers and their children do fine. But the odds are stacked against them. Nearly three-fourths of children in single-parent families will experience poverty by age 11, as against only about a fifth of children in two-parent families. Cohabitation appears to be less stable than marriage, even after other factors are accounted for. Research by the ton finds that children raised in single-parent homes are at greater risk of poverty, school dropout, delinquency, teen pregnancy, and adult joblessness.

All those problems disproportionately affect blacks, but before you decide that race, rather than marriage, is the active ingredient in the witch's brew, consider a few other points. First, poverty correlates more strongly with a family's marital status than with its race. According to Census Bureau data, a two-parent black household is more likely to be poor than is a two-parent white household, but both are far less likely to be poor than is a mother-only household of either race. In other words, if you are a baby about to be born, your best odds are to choose married black parents over unmarried white ones.

Second, recent research finds that, dire though the consequences of single parenthood often are for black children, the consequences tend to be even worse for white children. "The consequences of family disruption are smaller for disadvantaged black and Hispanic children than for disadvantaged white children, both in terms of percentage points and in terms of proportionate effects," write Sara McLanahan and Gary Sandefur in their 1994 book, *Growing Up With a Single Parent: What Hurts, What Helps.* They add that a middle-class income is no shield. "The chances that a white girl from an advantaged background will become a teen mother is five times as high, and the chances a white child will drop out of high school is three times as high, if the parents do not live together."

> **❝** *Children of unwed parents are more likely to become unwed parents themselves.* **❞**

This is not to say that most children in single-parent families become teenage parents or drop out; most don't. It is to say that the long-term presence of two parents—in other words, marriage—is a better predictor of a child's life chances than is race or income, and that illegitimacy and single parenthood are risky no matter what your race or income. Indeed, Sawhill notes that the proliferation of single-parent households accounts for virtually all of the increase in child poverty since the early 1970s.

Other things being equal, unmarried parenthood tends to propagate itself. Children of unwed parents are more likely to become unwed parents themselves. The problem becomes even more severe when children grow up in whole communities where marriage is more the exception than the rule. Sawhill notes that in some of the country's biggest cities, and even a few states, a majority of all children (not just black children) are born out of wedlock. There are large areas, in other words, where marriage may seem as exotic as lawn tennis. Perhaps partly as a result, about half of American high school seniors now say that having a child without being married is experimenting with a worthwhile lifestyle choice or does not affect anyone else. Anything so common, after all, must be normal.

The Marriage Problem

No one knows what all this portends, but it would be foolish not to consider the possibility that America's families and children may be splitting into two increasingly divergent and self-perpetuating streams—two social classes, in other words—with marriage as the dividing line. Some children would grow up in a culture where marriage is taken for granted and parents worry about sport utility vehicles and quality day care, others in a culture where marriage is a pipe dream and deadbeat dads and impoverished kids are the norm. Ominously, in her research Sawhill finds that more American children today than in the 1970s have either very good or very poor life prospects, and fewer are in the middle. "There is a bifurcation in children's life prospects that threatens to divide the U.S. into a society of haves and have-nots," she writes.

Suppose, as all this evidence suggests, that what afflicts America is no longer first and foremost a poverty problem or a race problem but, rather, a marriage problem. Then neither income-based remedies such as welfare nor race-based remedies such as affirmative action will hit the mark. But what might a marriage-based remedy look like? "We don't have a clue how to get people married," Sawhill says. Theodora Ooms, the director of the Center for Law and Social Policy's marriage resource center, agrees. "This area is so new for social policy that we have no track record of research, demonstrations, evaluations," she says. "We're jump-starting the public policy debate" before either science or the public is prepared.

Still, the only way to find the right answers is to start asking the right questions. Every day, it becomes clearer that the old lenses of poverty and race are out of focus. The welfare reauthorization debate is a chance to begin looking at the world through a better pair of spectacles.

11
Capitalist Democracies Create Growing Inequality

Ian Shapiro

Ian Shapiro is a professor of political science at Yale University and a prominent theorist of democracy and justice. He is also the author of Democratic Justice.

As economic inequality continues to grow, social mobility has become an impossible dream for many. In a representative democracy, one would expect voters to favor taxing the rich in order to redistribute wealth and narrow the gap between rich and poor. However, democracies are in general tolerating growing inequality. The main reason for this phenomenon is that people in a lower stratum of society find it impossible to aspire to the wealth possessed by those in the upper classes. For example, a gardener or housekeeper could not imagine living in the same sort of mansion in which his or her employer resides. In the United States people tend to accept that the market is a fair and level playing field and that differences in income and wealth are also fair. In addition, members of the middle class are reluctant to seek changes in the economic system that would redistribute wealth because they fear that any alteration could threaten their own economic standing.

To ask why there is so much inequality in modern-day democracies is to ask a loaded question. Why should we expect there to be less?

Ian Shapiro, "Why the Poor Don't Soak the Rich," *Daedalus*, vol. 131, Winter 2002, pp. 118–28. Copyright © 2002 by the American Academy of Arts and Sciences. Reproduced by permission.

Such an expectation was nevertheless widely shared in the nineteenth century, both among conservatives who feared the economic implications of democracy and among socialists who welcomed democracy precisely because of its apparent economic implications. The Left and Right agreed: if majority rule and universal suffrage were introduced into a society marked by massive inequality, then most voters, being relatively poor, would inevitably favor taxing the rich and transferring the proceeds downward. I will call this the redistributive thesis.

This is one thesis that history has roundly refuted. Although there have been redistributive eras in capitalist democracies since the advent of a universal franchise, there has been no systematic relationship between democracy and downward redistribution—not even a detectable relationship between the expansions of the franchise and episodes of downward redistribution.

> If the gap between where a person is and where he or she might hope to be is too great, certain goods are likely to seem out of reach—and hence outside the range of realistic aspirations.

Indeed, expanding the franchise has sometimes been accompanied by regressive redistribution. In the United States, economic inequality rose sharply between early 1975 and the mid-1990s, despite the passage of the Voting Rights Act of 1965[1] and the lowering of the voting age to eighteen in 1971. Similarly, in the post-communist world, the advent of democracy has been accompanied by the ostentatious growth of inequality. No doubt these developments owe at least as much to the introduction of capitalism as they do to democracy. Still, if the redistributive thesis is of interest, it must surely predict that a representative democracy will reverse—or at least retard—the regressive implications of market capitalism. Yet in practice, democracies often seem willing to tolerate growing inequality.

There are several ways that social scientists have tried to explain this apparent anomaly. A number of them have pointed to the logic of democracy, the logic of capitalism, and the ways

1. The Voting Rights Act of 1965 was signed into law by President Johnson. It banned literacy tests or a denial of the right to vote on account of race.

in which they interact. Such analysts argue that the propensity to demand downward redistribution would be realized were it not for unexpected dynamics unleashed by the institutions of democracy and capitalism and their interaction.

My purpose here is not to criticize this kind of institutional account, but rather to raise doubts about some assumptions behind it. No doubt part of the intuitive plausibility of the redistributive thesis is that it seems supported by a number of common assumptions about human psychology. If individuals in general were rational in the pursuit of self-interest, or rational in their pursuit of class interests, then we would expect most people in a democracy to support downward redistribution—if not to the point of perfect economic equality, then at least to something a lot closer to it than what we now have.

The expectation that democracies will redistribute downward is often motivated by the observation of poverty amid opulence. It seems reasonable to anticipate that the greater the manifest opulence of the few, the stronger will be the redistributive pressure from below.

Paradoxically, however, something closer to the opposite may often be the case.

Why this discrepancy? An important part of the answer, I think, lies in exposing a number of dubious assumptions about human psychology. Those who adhere to the redistributive thesis, be they Marxist, liberal, or conservative, usually assume that people in general keep themselves well informed about their place in the distribution of income and wealth, that the poor and middle classes compare themselves to the wealthy when thinking about what is feasible or just, and that those toward the bottom of the income distribution are like coiled springs—were it not for various external forces that are pressing them down, they would leap into action and demand a greater share of the economic pie.

Every one of these assumptions is questionable—and every one of them deserves to be questioned.

Out of Reach

Aspirations do not form in vacuums. People must be able to picture realistically the goods for which they will strive. If the gap between where a person is and where he or she might hope to be is too great, certain goods are likely to seem out of reach—and hence outside the range of realistic aspirations. There thus arises the possibility of an empathy gulf, a situation in which people who are situated in one stratum of society may find it literally impossible to imagine the goods pursued by those in another.

When levels of inequality are extremely high, such an empathy gulf might actually dampen redistributive demands from the very poor. An extreme example will make this point. In modern-day Cape Town [in South Africa], it is common for domestic cleaners who live in squatters' camps to work for ten dollars a day cleaning half-million dollar houses, where the cars in the garages cost many multiples of their expected lifetime earnings. It may just be impossible for the cleaners to picture themselves ever owning such a car, let alone the houses in which their owners live. You can see yourself stepping unaided over a puddle or a stream, perhaps even swimming a river, but not swimming the Atlantic ocean.

> *In the United States, at least, although people might be egalitarian in many facets of social life, they tend to accept economic outcomes as legitimate unless they seem to be both procedurally and substantively unfair.*

By the same token, those who are very rich may find it impossible to picture themselves ever becoming poor. To the degree that willingness to tolerate downward redistribution is part of the worry "there but for the grace of God go I," the worry has to be credible. If you are rich and the gap between you and the poor you see around you is so vast that no calamity you can imagine befalling you will put you into their circumstances, then any prudential reasons you might have for improving their lot disappear. Presumably this is one reason why most people can tune out panhandlers and street people and acquiesce in the demonization of the underclass. The mighty may fall into destitution in [French novelist Emile] Zola's novels—but no one who reads Zola in modern-day America really expects that such things could happen to them.

The more extreme the income inequality, the greater the psychic distance between the have-nots and the haves. Beyond certain thresholds that would have to be determined empirically, inequality may be expected to spawn empathy gulfs that dampen demands for change from below and reinforce the complacency of those who are rich. If the conditions for revolutionary social change are absent, and if a democratic order is seen as fundamentally legitimate, then the very existence of a vast gulf between rich and poor may very well reinforce the inegalitarian status quo. People will be more likely to blame others who are close to themselves in the social order for their plight rather than the wealthy, who seem unimaginably far away. This may fuel characteristic types of conflict among different groups and classes toward the lower end of the socioeconomic spectrum, but it is unlikely to have much effect on the overall distribution of income and wealth.

The existence of empathy gulfs complements other possibilities that have been suggested to explain why voters would not make the kinds of egalitarian demands predicted by the redistributive thesis. An older sociology literature that runs from Max Weber to Frank Parkin suggests that in market systems most people think there is less inequality than there actually is, and that their relative position is better than it actually is. There is also an economics literature that seeks to explain people's apparently irrational beliefs about the prospects for their own upward mobility, and there is empirical research in social psychology that supports the notion that in formally egalitarian systems people opt for individual advancement rather than collective action to improve their circumstances.

In the United States, at least, although people might be egalitarian in many facets of social life, they tend to accept economic outcomes as legitimate unless they seem to be both procedurally and substantively unfair. But this seldom happens, because the market is widely believed to be a fair distributive instrument. Jennifer Hochschild's 1995 study, *Facing up to the American Dream: Race, Class, and the Soul of the Nation*, revealed a remarkably widespread endorsement of the idea that "skill rather than need should determine wages," and that "America should promote equal opportunity for all" rather than "equal outcomes." Overwhelming majorities from different occupational, racial, and political groups endorsed this ideology.

To be sure, not everyone believes in the justness of capitalism or the American Dream. Hochschild herself notes that a subset of the population is estranged from it. Because desolation and apathy are unlikely to coexist with ambition and determination for success, it seems clear that differently situated poor people have different beliefs and aspirations. It may be that those who could organize for redistributive politics are insufficiently disaffected to do so, while those who are sufficiently disaffected are incapable of organizing.

Bootstrap Ideology

Like empathy gulfs, what some psychologists call framing effects also shape what people see as pertinent political alternatives. Here the concern is not with the goods people might in principle, or on reflection, imagine themselves deciding to pursue, but rather with what they actually focus on when making a particular decision.

In 1984, Ronald Reagan ran for reelection by asking a pointed question: "Are you better off than you were four years ago?" This directed people to think about a bundle of goods represented by their disposable income, and to ask whether their stock of it had increased. This is a self-referential comparison: it requires no attention to what others have.

Research shows that people often think largely in self-referential terms. Moreover, when they do compare themselves to others, it is generally to people who are situated like themselves. Workers do not compare themselves to their bosses in assessing their circumstances. They do not compare themselves to the rich, but rather to workers like themselves.

Yet even if most workers understand their own interest in such narrow terms, it still seems to follow that workers pursuing the interests they do share will, sooner or later, support a redistribution of wealth—this, after all, was a part of what [Communist philosopher] Karl Marx expected to happen under capitalism. To explain why this does not happen, we should attend to a variety of other factors.

For example, one reason workers might not press for redistribution stems from backward-looking framing effects, a phrase meant to capture the reactive character of much human behavior. After all, the query "Are you better off than you were four years ago?" directs attention to the past—with the implication that the alternative to the present is not progress, but backsliding. Once a marginal advance has occurred, there is always the possibility of losing it.

People who are surprised that there are not more demands for downward redistribution tend to work on the assumption that those near the bottom of the economic distribution think they have nothing to lose. This may be true for a handful of people, but certainly not for most—and definitely not for most modern-day workers. In many circumstances, voters may decide that things could well get worse—particularly if things have been worse in the recent past.

What may be called inward-looking framing effects also shape the decisions that people routinely make. Rallying grassroots supporters for the Million Man March in October of 1995, [Nation of Islam leader] Louis Farrakhan insisted that the time had come for the dispossessed in the black community to draw on their own resources and bootstrap themselves out of poverty. His message was unequivocal: forget the inequality out there and focus on yourself. When people internalize ideologies of this kind, they will not demand redistribution through public institutions. Instead, they will blame themselves for their circumstances and accept that they should look inward when trying to improve them. Inward-looking framing effects are likely significant in accounting for the dearth of redistributive demands in the United States, given the power of bootstrapping ideologies here. Whether the inward-looking focus is on the self or on a comparatively dispossessed group, it is significantly not on the larger society and its distribution of goods and opportunities.

> *// Even individuals who are fully aware of the real dimensions of economic inequality sometimes decide that they have other priorities that are more important than trying to redress perceived economic injustice. //*

Even individuals who are fully aware of the real dimensions of economic inequality sometimes decide that they have other priorities that are more important than trying to redress perceived economic injustice. Some people may be more concerned about their status or dignity than about income and wealth. In contemporary South Africa, for instance, the abolition of second-class citizenship since the democratic transition in 1994 has produced a tangible new noneconomic good: the dignity that comes with the act of voting. In such circumstances, the mere right to vote may well dampen popular concern with the continuing existence of economic inequality.

Even in the United States, economic issues must vie for attention with concerns about status and recognition. Part of the appeal of ethnic and other forms of identity politics in countries like ours comes from the persistence of status inequalities. By focusing on issues of status and dignity, social movements sometimes draw attention away from more purely economic concerns.

Fear of the Underclass

Downward-looking framing effects draw attention away from redistribution in still another way: by directing attention to those less fortunate in the social order. The existence of the very poor can seem frightening to those just above them in the social order in at least three ways: they might be thought to threaten violence, they might be believed to be the cause of tax burdens to fund welfare demands, and the possibility of unemployment might conjure up the possibility of plunging into their ranks.

Fear of the marauding rabble of dispossessed poor has existed for centuries. Rather than disappearing in capitalist democracies like the United States, this fear seems to have taken on a petit bourgeois form. Among those in the middle class and especially the lower middle class the fear takes the form of an antipathy toward those who are below them. There is even a tendency for those in the upper reaches of the lower class to distance themselves from the lower reaches, identifying instead with middle-class norms.

At the same time, a good deal of electoral politics in a modern democracy revolves around reinforcing stereotyped images of the underclass in ways that foment tensions between working-class and upper-middle-class Americans. Much of the trench warfare around affirmative action, for instance, is about promotions in the police department, the post office, and the fire department. It has little impact on people who live in Scarsdale [New York] or on the structure of income distribution. This is why political commentator Michael Lind can write of a white upper middle class, whose members support racial preferences and multiculturalism from which they are largely immune, that they "live right and think left" by looking askance at lower-middle-class opposition to their preferred policies. Though Lind perhaps exaggerates when he argues that affirmative action is the result of a divide-and-conquer conspiracy, he is surely right about its effects: keeping America's middle and lower classes squabbling among themselves feeds racism and destroys what otherwise might be natural political alliances in a campaign for redistributive change.

Downward-looking framing effects are sustained by demonizing those at or near the bottom of the social order. Hatred of welfare stems from the perception that most recipients are undeserving. Media portrayals of the very poor as disproportionately black and lazy reinforce this perception—as does the act of criminalizing the poor. The vast numbers of poor people who currently are housed in American prisons constitute a manifestly demonized group—even though the overwhelming majority of these prisoners have in fact committed no violent crime.

Political Distractions

Finally, perceptions of political alternatives are often shaped by anecdotal distractions. In *Albion's Fatal Tree*, historian Douglas Hay tells the story of an eighteenth-century criminal law that operated almost exclusively in the interests of propertied elites, but by means of which even noblemen were occasionally subjected to extreme forms of punishment—even the death penalty—for relatively minor offenses against property. Hay argues that such token but spectacular punishments meted out to aristocrats were meant to instill awe for the legal order that protected the propertied classes. What better way to get the poor to think that the law is not the instrument of the rich than to have it so visibly enforced against a member of the nobility?

Anecdotal distractions need not be directed only at the rich: lurid stories about "welfare queens" driving Cadillacs draw attention away from the law-abiding behavior of most welfare recipients. Horatio Alger stories [about rags-to-riches successes] work in the same way, as Ronald Reagan well understood ("What I want to see above all is that this country remains a country where someone can always get rich"). When politicians visibly single out individuals who have moved from welfare to work or otherwise triumphed over adversity, they exhibit their understanding of the power of anecdotal distractions. The man in the street does not ask questions about random sampling or selecting on the dependent variable. . . .

As I have noted briefly in relation to the United States, and as others have detailed more systematically in connection with other countries, distributive politics have moved in different directions at different times in different democratic systems. Some of the factors adduced here apply generally, but some do not.

This can scarcely be surprising. The psychology of citizens is but one of a host of factors that influence the evolving structure of inequality in capitalist democracies. It may also be that democracies do redistribute downward sometimes, but that capitalist economies produce inequality at a faster rate than the political process can attenuate it. If so, a definitive evaluation of the redistributive thesis may prove elusive.

The past thirty years have been a period of unusually regressive redistribution in the United States. This suggests that we should look to historically contingent factors to account for it in addition to considering the ongoing obstacles to progressive redistribution that I have described. Among those mentioned here, two candidates are the advent of segmented democracy and the massive increase in the rate of incarceration for nonviolent crimes. Other dynamics I have mentioned may also have been involved, such as the paradoxical ways in which massive inequality may make downward redistribution more difficult once certain thresholds have been passed. Perhaps these developments are causally implicated in the upward redistribution we have seen in the United States in recent decades; perhaps they are consequences of it.

12

Forced Economic Redistribution Would Cause Greater Long-Term Poverty

Kevin A. Hassett

Kevin A. Hassett is the director of economic policy studies at the American Enterprise Institute and a former senior economist at the Federal Reserve Board. He is also the author of Dow 36,000.

Economic inequality challenges a nation's sense of social justice. However, any government intervention to redistribute a nation's wealth is counterproductive. Tax policies that penalize the rich in order to narrow inequalities will deter ingenuity and entrepreneurship. If entrepreneurs are discouraged from starting new businesses because of highly redistributive taxes, fewer jobs will be available for poor people. If instead societies abandon the pursuit of economic equality and encourage the freedom to innovate, economies grow and poor people benefit.

As the 2004 campaign begins in earnest, it appears the Democrats' preferred strategy will be to tie a weak economy to President [George W.] Bush's economic policies. But what will they talk about if the economy gets strong? Several pieces in the *New York Times* suggest the answer: income inequality. The best example is a *Times Magazine* piece by Paul Krugman contending

Kevin A. Hassett, "Rich Man, Poor Man: How to Think About Income Inequality (Hint: It's Not as Bad as You May Think)," *National Review*, vol. 55, June 16, 2003. Copyright © 2003 by National Review, Inc., 215 Lexington Ave., New York, NY 10016. Reproduced by permission.

that we are entering a new Gilded Age [a time of great wealth in America] as "extravagant as the original." He recounts anecdotes of truly awe-inspiring wealth, of executives being treated like "royalty," and reports that in 1998 the 13,000 richest families had about the same combined income as the 20 million poorest households. The data are pretty striking, and reveal that income is far more concentrated at the top than it used to be. What should one do about it? Yale's Robert Shiller, writing in the *Times* op-ed section, proposed a law that would automatically increase tax rates on the wealthy if inequality increases.

Such drastic measures might be advisable if inequality were demonstrably harmful. But is it? I recently coedited (with [Bush economic adviser] R. Glenn Hubbard) a volume, *Inequality and Tax Policy*, that pulled together the leading research on the economics of inequality. One chapter in our book, contributed by Robert Barro of Harvard, found that inequality has a fairly unusual relationship with economic growth. If inequality is very high in a very poor nation, that country is likely to have low growth; but in wealthy, developed nations such as ours, economies have tended to do better when inequality is higher. And there is certainly no evidence that inequality results in political upheaval in such democracies: If we gave Bill Gates an extra $50 billion, it would not have a predictable effect on the typical voter's life.

> *If we redistribute now we may make some folks better off today, but we may also undermine economic growth and create an authoritarian government that opposes our freedoms.*

Inequality matters to the voter mostly to the extent that it affects his sense of the basic justice of society. Many of the inequalities arise because of choices. Workers with unpleasant jobs are often compensated for that unpleasantness with a higher wage. But other forms of inequality, such as abject poverty, may also be the result of misfortune. In this area, redistributive arguments appear quite compelling: Hungry children will be fed everywhere if only we roll back President Bush's tax cuts.

But the president would be right to insist on the tax cuts. Consider an example first suggested by [economist] Milton

Friedman in his landmark book *Capitalism and Freedom* that I take some liberties with here. Imagine a small tropical archipelago with three islands. We drop one individual on each island, and each faces dramatically different circumstances. One of the islands is densely forested with fruit and coconut trees and provides a pleasurable life of leisure to its inhabitant. Another has sufficient fish in its lagoons to provide sustenance, but only to a hard-working fisherman. The third is a barren wasteland, and the poor individual who lands there can barely survive by eating insects.

The Problem of Forced Redistribution

Now imagine that you have been appointed governor of this archipelago. Should you move everyone to the nice island? Should you seize resources from the lucky fellow and give them to the insectivore? A typical response might be that the different outcomes are purely the result of luck, and hence have no moral standing. Government could enter and make the poor better off—and is justified in doing so, since the wealthy fellow would want there to be redistribution if he had landed on a different island.

If this example is not extreme enough to arouse such a response in you, then let's revise it to try to change your mind. Suppose that a young child lands on the bad island and will die if we do not take some food from the good island. Should government act now?

So there are cases where inequality is a worthy motivation for government action. But before we book our flight to Sweden, let's change the scenario again. Suppose that each island is identical, with arable land but little else. One fellow builds a palatial farm and dines on fine foods grown on his property. The other two do not develop their islands, but sit around enjoying the beach all day, sustaining themselves with insects. Given the different circumstances, has your favored government policy changed? A typical answer might be that the lazy beachcombers don't deserve the hard-earned fruits of the farmer and should be left to their bugs.

In the real world, differences emerge between citizens because of both luck and choices. Virtually every circumstance is a mixture of these two cases. This distinction is important, because it makes it difficult if not impossible to conceive of scenarios where justice clearly supports forceful redistribution.

Moreover, since effort is almost always part of the picture, it is likely that redistribution will be counterproductive even from the perspective of the poor. After all, governments play a dynamic game. If we take away the fruits of effort today in the name of social justice, there will be fewer fruits tomorrow. If we discourage entrepreneurs from starting new businesses today with our highly redistributive taxes, then tomorrow's poor might not be able to find a job and could well go hungry.

The Importance of Freedom

These concerns are magnified if governments are potentially corrupt. If a person yields a portion of his freedom to government, how can he be sure that other freedoms will not also be lost? There is no guarantee that we would not all end up with absolutely equal incomes locked away in a gulag.

Thus the question of social justice is an empirical one. If we redistribute now we may make some folks better off today, but we may also undermine economic growth and create an authoritarian government that opposes our freedoms. Nobody wants to live in a world of hungry children, but which view of the world leads to the policy that produces the fewest cries over time?

> *Freedom wins because it is desirable in itself and because its presence has so soundly advanced social justice.*

From a global perspective, the evidence is quite clear: Freedom wins. Columbia economist Xavier Sala-i-Martin recently published a paper that carefully explored the evolution of world poverty and income inequality over time. He found that inequality and poverty have declined sharply, with the steepest decline occurring after 1980 (a year that may sound familiar to Reaganites). The figures are striking: The number of individuals with a real income below $2 a day dropped about 40 percent (affecting 400 million individuals) between 1980 and 2000. Why the big shift? Sala-i-Martin found that the movement of many countries (especially China) away from socialism and toward free-market capitalism had a profound effect on economic growth and the welfare of the poor. As societies abandoned the pursuit of absolute equality in favor of the pursuit of liberty, growth emerged and the poor benefited.

On a different scale of poverty, it is also true that the Western European nations with large welfare states have had abysmal economic records—with the bigger socialist nations, France and Germany, posting economic growth over the past decade about 1 percentage point below that of the U.S. Compound that difference for decades and even folks in the bottom of the U.S. income distribution will be better off than the typical Frenchman. So which society will deliver a better life to the poor?

At the micro level, one will always be able to find individual cases that challenge conservative dogma. Ten years from now, many fewer people will live in poverty if growth-oriented tax policies are enacted—but confiscatory taxes could undoubtedly address evils that exist today. My colleague Robert Hahn has calculated that, statistically speaking, an extra 40 years of life could be provided to some U.S. citizen if life-saving government programs were increased by $3.8 million. Accordingly, one could conceivably give 40 years of life to 10,504 Americans by confiscating Bill Gates's income and dedicating it all to targeted government programs. Posed that way, how could one allow Mr. Gates to keep his money?

Of course, the problem is solved if private charity arises without the coercion of government, and Mr. Gates has an excellent record in that regard. But if we leave that aside, conservatives are left defending unfettered capitalism with the argument that it produces a world in which 400 million individuals worldwide can rise permanently above poverty in just a few decades, in part because transitory fixes are eschewed. This position is sound, but even Friedman had difficulty with the trade-off: "The fact that these arguments against the capitalist ethic are invalid does not of course demonstrate that the capitalist ethic is an acceptable one. I find it difficult to justify either accepting or rejecting it, or to justify any alternative principle. I am led to the view that it cannot in and of itself be regarded as an ethical principle; that it must be regarded as instrumental or a corollary of some other principle such as freedom."

Freedom wins because it is desirable in itself and because its presence has so soundly advanced social justice. Defending it requires dogged reference to long-run goods that far outweigh the benefits of quick fixes.

Organizations to Contact

The editors have compiled the following list of organizations concerned with the issues debated in this book. The descriptions are derived from materials provided by the organizations. All have publications or information available for interested readers. The list was compiled on the date of publication of the present volume; the information provided here may change. Be aware that many organizations take several weeks or longer to respond to inquiries, so allow as much time as possible.

American Enterprise Institute (AEI)
1150 Seventeenth St. NW, Washington, DC 20036
(202) 862-5800 • fax: (202) 862-7177
Web site: www.aei.org

The American Enterprise Institute is a public policy institute that sponsors research and provides commentary on a wide variety of issues, including economics, social welfare, and government tax and regulatory policies. It publishes the bimonthly magazine *American Enterprise* and the *AEI Newsletter*.

Cato Institute
1000 Massachusetts Ave. NW, Washington, DC 20001-5403
(202) 842-0200 • fax: (202) 842-3490
Web site: www.cato.org

The Cato Institute is a libertarian public policy research foundation dedicated to promoting traditional American principles of limited government, individual liberty, and peace. The institute advocates abolishing all government welfare programs and returning charity to the private sector. It publishes the triannual *Cato Journal*, the bimonthly newsletter *Cato Policy Report*, and the quarterly magazine *Regulation*.

Coalition on Human Needs (CHN)
1000 Wisconsin Ave. NW, Washington, DC 20007
(202) 342-0726 • fax: (202) 342-1132
Web site: www.chn.org

The coalition is a federal advocacy organization that works to address the needs of low-income and other vulnerable people. It lobbies for adequate federal funding for welfare, Medicaid, and other social services. CHN's publications include its *Human Needs Report* newsletter, which is published bimonthly when Congress is in session, and issue briefs on various topics, including the minimum wage, child nutrition, and Medicaid.

Economic Policy Institute (EPI)
1600 L St. NW, Suite 1200
Washington, DC 20036
(202) 775-8810 • fax: (202) 775-0819
Web site: www.epinet.org

The Economic Policy Institute conducts research and provides a forum for the exchange of information on economic policy. It promotes educational programs to encourage discussion of economic policy and economic issues, particularly the economics of poverty, unemployment, inflation, American industry, international competitiveness, and problems of economic adjustment as they affect the community and the individual. EPI publishes the *EPI Journal* and the biennial *State of Working America*.

Finance Project
1401 New York Ave. NW, Suite 800, Washington, DC 20005
(202) 587-1000 • fax: (202) 628-4205
e-mail: fininfo@financeproject.org • Web site: www.financeproject.org

The Finance Project is a nonprofit policy research, technical assistance, and information organization that seeks to help economically disadvantaged families. The organization publishes a wide array of reports, working papers, and strategy briefs on issues related to child welfare, workforce development, health care, and community and economic development.

Foundation for Economic Education
30 S. Broadway, Irvington, NY 10533
(914) 591-7230 • fax: (914) 591-8910
e-mail: freeman@fee.org • Web site: www.fee.org

The foundation publishes information and commentary in support of private property, the free market, and limited government. It frequently publishes articles on capitalism and conservatism in its monthly magazine the *Freeman*.

Heritage Foundation
214 Massachusetts Ave. NE, Washington, DC 20002
(202) 546-4400 • fax: (202) 546-8328
Web site: www.heritage.org

The foundation is a conservative public policy research institute dedicated to the principles of free, competitive enterprise, limited government, individual liberty, and a strong national defense. It advocates serious reform of the welfare system in such areas as controlling rising welfare costs and reducing illegitimacy. Among the foundation's numerous publications are the quarterly journal *Policy Review*, the book *The Road to Prosperity: Twenty-first Century Approach to Economic Development*, and the report *The Brutal Price of a Dollar*.

HUD USER
U.S. Department of Housing and Urban Development
PO Box 6091, Rockville, MD 20849
(800) 245-2691 • fax: (202) 708-9981
e-mail: helpdesk@huduser.org • Web site: www.huduser.org

HUD USER is a research information service and clearinghouse for people working toward improving housing and strengthening community development. It collects, develops, and distributes housing-related information. The organization publishes many reports related to housing and the economy, which are available on its Web site.

National Center for Children in Poverty
215 W. 125th St., 3rd Fl., New York, NY 10027
(646) 284-9600 • fax: (646) 284-9623
e-mail info@nccp.org • Web site: www.nccp.org

The National Center for Children in Poverty is a nonprofit public policy research institute whose mission is to identify and promote strategies that reduce child poverty in the United States. The institute publishes fact sheets and reports about issues related to child poverty, which are available on its Web site.

National Student Campaign Against Hunger and Homelessness (NSCAHH)
218 D St. SE, Washington, DC 20003
(202) 546-8195 • fax: (202) 546-2461
Web site: www.nscahh.org

The National Student Campaign Against Hunger and Homelessness is a public interest research group that works with coalitions of students and community members across the country to end hunger and homelessness through education, service, and action. The NSCAHH is the largest student network fighting hunger and homelessness in the country. The group publishes a variety of reports on homelessness, hunger, and affordable housing.

Progressive Policy Institute (PPI)
600 Pennsylvania Ave. SE, Suite 400, Washington, DC 20003
(202) 547-0001 • fax: (202) 544-5014
Web site: www.ppionline.org

The Progressive Policy Institute is a nonprofit research and education institute that seeks to accelerate economic growth in the United States, strengthen American families, and empower the urban poor. PPI publishes the books *Building the Bridge: 10 Big Ideas to Transform America* and *Mandate for Change,* as well as *Blueprint Magazine* and a variety of e-newsletters.

Reason Foundation
3415 S. Sepulveda Blvd., Suite 400, Los Angeles, CA 90034
(310) 391-2245 • fax: (310) 391-4395
Web site: www.reason.org

The foundation works to provide a better understanding of the intellectual basis of a free society and to develop new ideas in public policy making. It researches contemporary social, economic, urban, and political problems. The foundation believes that welfare has become a destructive, multigenerational lifestyle that burdens working Americans with higher taxes. It publishes the newsletter *Privatization Watch* monthly and *Reason* magazine eleven times a year.

Welfare Law Center
275 Seventh Ave., Suite 1205, New York, NY 10001-6708
(212) 633-6967 • fax: (212) 633-6371
e-mail: hn0135@handsnet.org • Web site: www.welfarelaw.org

The center is a nonprofit organization that works to ensure that adequate income support is available to meet the basic needs of the poor, including poor children. It publishes the monthly *Welfare Bulletin*, the bimonthly *Welfare News*, and a variety of reports on issues related to welfare. These publications are available on its Web site.

Bibliography

Books

James Auerbach and Richard S. Belous, eds.	*The Inequality Paradox: The Growth of Income Disparity.* Washington, DC: National Policy Association, 1998.
Joel Blau	*Illusions of Prosperity: Working Families in an Age of Economic Insecurity.* Oxford, UK: Oxford University Press, 1999.
Dennis Duane Braun	*The Rich Get Richer: The Rise of Income Inequality in the United States and the World.* Chicago: Nelson-Hall, 1997.
Steve Brouwer	*Sharing the Pie: A Citizen's Guide to Wealth and Power in America.* New York: Henry Holt/Owl, 1998.
Grace Chang	*Disposable Domestics: Immigrant Women Workers in the Global Economy.* Cambridge, MA: South End Press, 2000.
Chuck Collins	*Shifting Fortunes: The Perils of the Growing American Wealth Gap.* Boston: United for a Fair Economy, 1999.
Richard Douthwaite	*The Growth Illusion: How Economic Growth Has Enriched the Few, Impoverished the Many, and Endangered the Planet.* Gabriola Island, Canada: New Society, 1999.
Ronald Dworkin	*Sovereign Virtue: The Theory and Practice of Equality.* Cambridge, MA: Harvard University Press, 2000.
Barbara Ehrenreich	*Nickel and Dimed: On (Not) Getting By in America.* New York: Metropolitan Books, 2001.
Robert Frank	*The Winner Take All Society: Why the Few at the Top Get So Much More than the Rest of Us.* New York: Penguin USA, 1996.
Philip Green	*Equality & Democracy.* New York: New Press, 1998.
Jody Heymann	*The Widening Gap: Why America's Working Families Are in Jeopardy and What Can Be Done About It.* New York: Basic Books, 2000.
Lisa Keister	*Wealth in America: Trends in Wealth Inequality.* Cambridge, UK: Cambridge University Press, 2000.

Ray F. Marshall — *Back to Shared Prosperity: The Growing Inequality of Wealth and Income in America.* New York: M.E. Sharpe, 1999.

Benjamin Page — *What Government Can Do: Dealing with Poverty and Inequality.* Chicago: University of Chicago Press, 2000.

Edward N. Wolff — *Top Heavy: The Increasing Inequality of Wealth in America and What Can Be Done About It.* New York: New Press, 1999.

Periodicals

Robert J. Bresler — "The Dilemma of Income Inequality," *USA Today Magazine,* May 2000.

David Callahan — "Take Back Values," *Nation,* February 2004.

Douglas Clement — "Beyond 'Rich' and 'Poor,'" *Region,* June 2003.

CQ *Researcher* — "At Issue: Are There Two Americas?" April 2005.

Sheldon Danziger — "Comment on 'The Age of Extremes: Concentrated Affluence and Poverty in the Twenty-first Century,'" *Demography,* November 1996.

Economist — "Ever Higher Society, Ever Harder to Ascend," January 2005.

David Futrelle, Jon Birger, and Pat Regnier — "Getting Rich in America: Who Says the American Dream Is Dead?" *Money,* May 1, 2005.

Ted Halstead — "The American Paradox," *Atlantic Monthly,* January 2003.

Kevin A. Hassett — "Rich Man, Poor Man: How to Think About Income Inequality (Hint: It's Not as Bad as You May Think)," *National Review,* June 16, 2003.

Nigel Holloway — "In Praise of Inequality," *Forbes,* March 2003.

Paul Krugman — "The Death of Horatio Alger: Our Political Leaders Are Doing Everything They Can to Fortify Class Inequality," *Nation,* January 5, 2004.

Stephen Moore — "Careful Whom You Soak," *National Review,* November 24, 2003.

Cait Murphy — "Are the Rich Cleaning Up?" *Fortune,* September 4, 2000.

Robert J. Samuelson — "Pushing Economic Equality Won't Work for U.S.," *Human Events,* May 1995.

Walter E. Schaller — "Rawls, the Difference Principle, and Economic Inequality," *Pacific Philosophical Quarterly,* December 1998.

Benjamin Schwarz — "Reflections on Inequality," *World Policy Journal,* Winter 1995–1996.

Janny Scott and
D. Leonhardt

"Class in America: Shadowy Lines That Still Divide," *New York Times*, May 15, 2005.

Christopher Shea

"American Economy Less Dynamic than Thought," *Chronicle of Higher Education*, January 1997.

Mortimer B.
Zuckerman

"So the Rich Get Richer?" *U.S. News & World Report*, May 2, 2005.

Index

104

106